W9-BOE-691

THE DARE SISTERS

THE DARE SISTERS

Jess Rinker

[Imprint]
MAKE YOUR MARK
New York

[Imprint]
MAKE YOUR MARK

A part of Macmillan Publishing Group, LLC
120 Broadway, New York, NY 10271

Library of Congress Cataloging-in-Publication Data is available.

ISBN 978-1-250-21338-9 (hardcover) / ISBN 978-1-250-21339-6 (ebook)

Our books may be purchased in bulk for promotional, educational, or business use. Please contact your local bookseller or the Macmillan Corporate and Premium Sales Department at (800) 221-7945 ext. 5442 or by email at MacmillanSpecialMarkets@macmillan.com.

Book design by Carolyn Bull

Imprint logo designed by Amanda Spielman

First edition, 2020

1   3   5   7   9   10   8   6   4   2

mackids.com

'Tis true this little book contains
Countless secrets and treasures untold:
Codes and keys, riddles and games
About shiny pirates' gold.

So, should you fail to heed due dates,
Or pilfer, and ruin sales—
Avast, scallywag! Lest ye suffer dark fates!
For dead men tell no tales.

For Dad, who first introduced me to the magic of Ocracoke
and
for Joe, my true treasure

X Marks the Spot

September 1996

I press the tip of the blade against the soft skin of my finger.

"I, Savannah Mae Dare, solemnly swear . . ."

"Is that a knife?" my older sister, Frankie, interrupts me for the third time. I sigh. The first was to ask why we had to go to Springer's Point Preserve, the big nature park near our house. The second was why we had to go where it was a hundred degrees to sit under a giant live oak with fire ants in the sand. I reminded her we live in North Carolina. On an island. It's all giant oaks and fire ants and sand, not air-conditioning and iced drinks and fluffy pillows.

Somewhere overhead a seagull cries. It's so hot, even in the shade. But I don't dare complain because I want to finish our pledges, and get changed out of the ugly

1

navy-blue dress that makes me look like a sailor. Not that I'd mind looking like a real sailor, just not one in an ugly blue dress. Mom said this was the best one to wear for Grandpa's funeral, so I didn't argue. But enough is enough.

"Yes, Frankie. It's a knife. Now be quiet." I start over. "I, Savannah Mae Dare, solemnly swear to be one of the three appointed guardians of . . ."

"I'm not pricking my finger for this," Frankie interrupts me for the fourth time, and crosses her arms. "You always want blood. You wanted us to prick our fingers when you made us swear not to tell Mom and Dad about trying to get the lighthouse ghost on camera. Which we never did, might I remind you."

"This is different." Leave it to Frankie to bring that up. Mom didn't make *her* wear a dress today. She's wearing black pants and a button-down shirt. She always gets her own way because she's the oldest. Although if I had to guess, I bet she's sweating way more than me right now.

"You get weirder every day, Sav," she says.

"Don't be a baby. It doesn't hurt."

"Do you know how much bacteria is on that thing?" She presses her lips together, hides her fingers under her arms, and shakes her head. "Nope. Not happening. And you're not pricking Jolene's finger either."

Our youngest sister, Jolene, looks at both of us with raised eyebrows, waiting to see which one of us will decide her fate. She's wearing a frilly pink princess costume that makes her very light blond hair look whiter than ever. She's six and gets away with more than Frankie and I put together.

"This is different because you need to think like a pirate." I poke my own finger with the blade before Frankie can stop me, and I finish my pledge as fast as I can: ". . . swear to be one of the three appointed guardians, for as long as I may live, in accordance with the Dare family legend."

"I'm pretty sure not all pirates signed things in blood," Frankie says.

"Only the coolest ones." Grinning, I hold up my finger so Frankie can get a good long look at my bravery.

"Ewwwww!" Jolene squeals. "You're bleeding! Don't get it on my dress!" She moves her knees away from me but sticks out her hand. "Now do mine." She holds her finger still with her other hand and squeezes her eyes tight.

"See?" I say. "Even the first grader can do it." I try to take Jolene's hand, but Frankie slaps my hand away. Sand flies everywhere. She always has to be so dramatic.

"Dad will kill you if you do that. Actually, Dad will kill *me* if you do that." Frankie grabs the knife and folds it closed.

"Hey! That's mine! Grandpa gave it to me!" I try to pull it back out of her hand but Frankie's thirteen and stronger.

"You'll get it back later," Frankie says as she sticks it in her pocket. "We're not pricking our fingers."

"Who put you in charge?" I ask.

"Dad, when he said, 'Frankie, since you're the biggest and the smartest, you're in charge. Don't let your little sisters cut themselves with rusty army knives.'"

"He didn't say that," Jolene says, giggling.

"It's from the navy, anyway," I mumble. Our grandpa was a hero in the navy, not the army. How could she forget that?

Frankie rolls her eyes. "Whatever. Dad put me in charge."

"How do you expect to be a right and true guardian if you can't even give your finger a tiny prick?"

"By using my brain," Frankie says, mocking my voice and pointing to her head. "I wouldn't expect you to understand since you don't have one."

I scramble to go after her, sending sand and leaves everywhere, but Jolene yells, "Y'all! We've got work to do! We have to stick together!"

She's right. I sit back down, grip a handful of sand, and let it slide through my palm. Grandpa always said we were stronger when we worked together. But it's hard sometimes with an athletic, popular older sister and a beauty queen baby sister. Only Grandpa understood me—he was the middle of three boys—and he was the only one I could talk to. All last year he walked with me to school and we'd talk about everything, but over the summer he got sick. And now he's gone.

I push my toes deep into the sand while my sisters examine the map and swat at mosquitoes starting to whine around us, circling our ears like they're trying to find a way in. Gulls continue to cry overhead. Waves crash onto the tiny beach at the end of the park, a constant *hushhh hushhh* we usually get so used to we don't hear it anymore. But the ocean always sounds louder at sunset and sunrise.

How pale and strange Grandpa had looked at the funeral. I try to shake the image out of my head. I'd rather think about Grandpa the way he was when he was alive. Grandpa loved history and maps. Way before I was born, he helped make maps for the navy and after that for people who treasure hunted like he did. He'd been all around the world, but loved Ocracoke the best. And he loved Springer's Point and used to take the three of us walking here all the time. He said there was magic here. Even though he'd been all over, his favorite stories were about the pirates, and about how Blackbeard died here.

"Blackbeard was misunderstood too," Grandpa had said, one afternoon after I'd gotten into an argument with a girl named Kate at school. We were best friends until she called me a weird show-off for knowing so many countries on the globe. And I pushed her into a garbage can.

"What do you mean?" I'd asked.

"Don't get me wrong. He was a pirate like all the rest. But mostly he got his reputation from acting dangerous and scary. People assumed he was a murderer and he let them believe it."

"Then they'd be so afraid of him he could rob them easier?"

"That's right." Grandpa looked at me seriously. "But you're not a pirate, Savvy. You don't need this reputation; it's not who you really are. What do you think about a parley with Kate? Even pirates sometimes called a truce."

"She called me 'chicken legs.'"

"Okay, maybe you're not ready for a parley. How else could you have handled it?"

Personally I thought pushing her into the garbage can was a pretty good solution. But I understood Grandpa's point. He gave me a big squeeze and we walked the beach to look for shells and gold coins. We only ever found shells.

But I know the coins are out there somewhere. I'll find them for Grandpa.

"Savannah?" Frankie waves her hand in front of my face.

Blotchy light through the gnarly oaks and dangling moss reminds me it's getting late.

"Sav, wrap this up. We have to be home before the

party or Dad's going to come looking," Frankie says like she's reading my mind.

"Or worse," I say, "send Peter to find us." Peter's our cousin and always has his nose in our business. He's a total snitch. I can't count how many times he's told on us to his parents and gotten us in trouble. I'm actually surprised he didn't see us sneaking away after Grandpa's funeral. Peter does not need to know about this. Grandpa didn't say his map was for all the cousins. Just us.

"Exactly," Frankie says. "So are we done?"

"You have to say your vows first. I did mine."

"Okay, but no blood."

"*Fine*. No blood."

I smooth Grandpa's map out between us, flick off a couple of ants, and let it slide that my sisters aren't going to prick their fingers. "Go ahead, Jolene," I say.

She raises her right hand like the Scouts. "Jolene Lee Dare promises to guard the map forever."

"Close enough," I say. "Frances?"

"Do not call me that."

"You have to use your full name or it's null and void."

"What's 'null and void'?" Jolene asks.

"Means it doesn't count," I say, leaning toward my big sister. "*Frances.*"

"I, Frances Elaine Dare, promise to be one of the three appointed guardians according to the Dare family legend."

"Perfect," I say, and gently roll Grandpa's map and stick it in the tube. When he got sick he told me it would be ours after he was gone. As much as I always loved looking at all the landmarks and Grandpa's cool handwriting on it, I didn't want to believe the day would ever come when that would happen. But it did. Last Wednesday, Grandpa passed away in his sleep. Dad said it was the best way, that Grandpa had no pain. Even though we did.

I know Grandpa would be proud of me for taking such good care of his map from here on out. I slide the tube in my backpack, and we all stand up and brush off the sand.

I put a hand on each of my sisters' shoulders. "We are now the official guardians of Cornelius Franklin Dare's Ocracoke Island map," I say. "The one and only way to find Blackbeard the Pirate's treasure."

Captain of the Kids' Table

When we come out of the park, we slip our shoes back on and walk home fast. It's not a long walk, but Mom and Dad are getting ready for a party to celebrate Grandpa's life and we want to be back before they realize we've been gone. If we had our skateboards we could move quicker, but for some reason Mom banned skateboards from the church.

We pass the old lighthouse and when our house is in sight, we see many extra bikes and a few cars parked out front. Most people walk or bike around the island. But we have some family and friends from the mainland who brought their cars over on the ferry. I run a stick down the iron fence that lines our property, which makes a soothing *tapatapatapatapatapa* sound, and then shove the stick upright in the sand by the porch.

A man wearing a green hat with a yellow anchor

pushes out our front door and nearly plows over Jolene as he comes down the steps. He looks surprised to see us, but quickly smiles and tips his hat. "Excuse me, lassies. I'm late for an appointment, but wanted to pay my respects to your family."

"Thank you," Frankie answers for all three of us. The man doesn't wait for any more response and just about jogs down the street.

"Who was that?" I ask. Frankie shrugs.

"He was at the church talking to Uncle Randy." Jolene jumps up each step with two feet.

"Maybe he was a friend of Grandpa's," Frankie says.

There's a wreath of flowers and a huge photo of Grandpa when he was younger and dressed in his US navy uniform by the front door. It was set up at the funeral, too, with an American flag folded up in a glass case. I didn't really look at it before but pause now. Grandpa's name and the dates 1910–1996 are written across the bottom. He used to brag that he'd make it to one hundred and be the oldest person in Ocracoke Village. I stare at it for a little while and think, *You almost made it, Grandpa,* until Frankie all but pushes me into the house.

Our parents, and our aunts and uncles and neighbors who came, are all too busy standing around the dining room table eating nasty deviled eggs to even notice us barge in on their conversation.

"Don't you remember when he sailed out of the Dry

Tortugas and came home with a plank of wood, declaring it to be a piece of history?" someone says. "And then the park service came knocking on his door a week later for removing it?"

Peter's parents, Uncle Randy and Aunt Della, are laughing so hard it looks like they might choke on an egg. One aunt I didn't even know before this morning, who came all the way from Atlanta, says, "He thought everything was treasure! What a nut, that old man! I mean, to give him credit, he found a lot of interesting things, but who actually thinks Blackbeard's treasure is real?"

"No one does, it's all folklore for the tourists," someone else says. "The man got confused in his later years."

"I think Cornelius was born confused."

And everyone laughs at Grandpa.

Except Mom and Dad. Probably because Grandpa was Dad's dad and we've been living with him since I was born. No one even came to visit him other than Uncle Randy and Aunt Della. It feels like he's more our family than everyone else's. And Grandpa was not confused. He knew more about Blackbeard than anyone. If he said there's a treasure, there's a treasure.

Jolene whispers, "Don't they know about the Dare family legend?"

I don't have the heart to tell her I made that part up.

Mom raises an eyebrow when she finally sees us. It's like her eyebrow is asking us where we've been, why we're late, and why we're covered in sand, *again*, but this is one of those times that we know we're not getting in trouble. I don't have any time to change out of this awful dress, though, because she points to the food. The three of us grab plates because we know what's good for us. Don't mess with Mom's eyebrow.

"Why are they making fun of Grandpa?" Jolene whispers, as Frankie piles dried-out baked ziti on Jolene's plate. The pastor's wife brought that. She brings it to every funeral.

And wedding.

And any potluck of any kind.

"They're not making fun of Grandpa," Frankie says, trying to comfort Jolene. But she looks at me because we both know the adults are *joking but not joking* in the way that adults do when they don't want to sound mean, but *are* being mean. She hands Jolene a fork and says, "Go sit."

Jolene spills half of her ziti as she walks to the little kids' table Dad set up for the younger cousins. Our dog, Py, short for "Pirate," cleans up after her as she goes. At the table, there's one more empty chair between her and another of our cousins, Peter's younger brother, Will, who's three and always throwing his food. There's no *way* I'm sitting there. I'm eleven. Way too old for that nonsense.

"I don't see what they find so funny," I whisper to Frankie as we fill our plates. "Grandpa found some of the most amazing treasures, and they all know it. He even has things at the historical society. Real artifacts from real shipwrecks." I pluck every single shrimp—twenty-three—from the serving platter and put them on my plate.

"Not everyone thinks it's all treasure," Frankie says. She puts four of my shrimps back. And then she helps herself to a disgusting-looking pasta salad. Anything with the word "salad" should be outlawed from family gatherings. That one's from Aunt Della, Peter's mom. She always uses those gross green olives with the strange little red things in them. I'm pretty sure they're bits of earlobe.

"Yuck. Don't eat that!" I try to swipe one off her plate.

"Mind your own food," she says.

"I'm trying to save your life," I say.

"Do you even know what that black line is on your shrimp?" she asks, grinning.

I stick my tongue out at her and then pop a shrimp into my mouth. Not as disgusting as earlobe salad.

I grab one more shrimp from the platter to make up for the one I ate and we both walk over to the dining table. Frankie sits down near Peter's oldest brother, Robbie, who's sixteen and can drive. He's the oldest of all the cousins. We hardly see him. And even Peter gets to sit at the dining table now that he just turned twelve. When I try to join them Dad says, "Sorry, kiddo, one more year on deck."

"Come on, Dad," I start to argue, but he looks so sad and tired. Plus there's a portrait of Grandpa behind him on the wall. I feel like it's staring at me. Grandma painted it when they were first married. Grandpa's a lot younger in the painting, and looks a lot like Dad when he smiles, but I can still picture Grandpa's expression, that way he'd tell me to "lower my sails," meaning calm down, without saying a word. A lot like Mom, actually. I wonder if he taught it to her. But since Grandpa's not here to give me that look, I have to stop myself from arguing with Dad.

"Thank you, Savvy," he says.

When I sit down at the kids' table I grumble, ignoring everything Grandpa used to tell me about trying to get along with others. "None of you better spill anything on me or I'm making you walk the plank," I announce.

Cheeks full of ziti, Jolene nods and salutes as if to confirm my status on this ship. She does that a lot when she thinks I'm getting too bossy. The rest of the cousins look at each other and then go back to eating. Will throws a pea at my face. If I have one more year at the kids' table, I'm going to have to start acting more like a pirate.

Blackbeard would never allow this treatment.

Queen Mary's Secrets

After most of the family and friends leave, it's only Peter's family and our family. Peter plays with the dog, while Will walks around eating things off the ground. Peter's dad, Uncle Randy, and our dad are brothers, and they never get along about anything, but they hang out all the time anyway. Kinda like me and Frankie, but louder, taller, man versions. Mom says Ocracoke is a small island and you get what you get.

Aunt Della and Mom are usually pretty good friends as long as Mom doesn't bring up her writing, because even though Mom writes really smart things like language textbooks, Aunt Della thinks she and Dad should help them with their family business. Aunt Della and Uncle Randy run fishing trips from their charter boat for all the vacationers that come to the village. They make a lot more money than my parents, but they usually smell like fish.

While Mom and Aunt Della talk and clean up in the kitchen, I follow Dad and Uncle Randy as they walk through the house, "taking inventory," as Uncle Randy says, whatever that means. They don't know I'm following them.

Uncle Randy holds up a copper vase. "A lot of this stuff will fetch a nice price at auction, Jack," he says. "You're going to have to let it go."

"I know, but it's Dad's life's work. How do I decide?" My dad rubs his face with his hands. I can tell he doesn't want to be having this conversation right now. Probably not ever. Grandpa's treasures cover the inside of our three-story house, which is really Grandpa's house and what he used to call the Queen Mary. He always told everyone our house was named after Grandma, but one day he told me a secret. He said it was also named after Mary Read, one of the most famous girl pirates ever. He said, like a ship, he wanted to name the house after an important woman. Or two. I asked him why did it have to be a girl's name and he said because, like Grandma, a woman takes you into her heart and she becomes your home. And for the pirates, their ship was their home.

I never understood all the stories Grandpa told me, but I liked the way he talked about Grandma, especially because I'd never met her. I also liked the way he talked about pirates. Which is why I decided to become one.

I just don't have a good pirate name yet. Most pirates have nicknames, like Blackbeard, whose real name was Edward Teach. I'm still working on mine.

The Queen Mary is unique in Ocracoke because there aren't many big, old houses like this on the island. Most are small or built on stilts to withstand hurricanes, but Grandpa always said our house was watched over by the ghosts of all the pirates who used to sail around Ocracoke, especially Blackbeard, and of course Mary Read and Grandma. We never had to worry because we had them as our guardian angels.

All kinds of things Grandpa found fill the rooms of our house in the same way another family might have a pile of magazines on the coffee table or framed art on the walls. But instead of everything coming from a store, it all came from the ocean. Besides some of the bigger things, like antique anchors and some strange metal devices with barnacles growing all over them, there are plenty of artifacts we're allowed to touch if we're very careful.

My favorite are the glass bubbly balls on the windowsills. I pick one up now and gently roll it in my hands as I walk by jars of unique seashells, fishing nets, old picture frames and portraits, driftwood, shards of pottery and jewelry in boxed glass cases, and shelves of old worn books about sailing and pirates, shelves that never get dusty. Grandpa's maps hang on nearly every wall. I love living here. It's like walking around a museum every day.

I can't believe Uncle Randy would want Dad to sell any of it.

I crouch behind the big piece of driftwood that we use as an umbrella stand near the stairs and think about Grandpa's map in my backpack. There's no way they're getting rid of the maps! Uncle Randy puts his hand on Dad's back and hands him a little card. "Call Throop. I know you were closer to the old man, that's why I'm leaving it to you to do, but you know what has to be done."

Dad nods. It might be the first time they've ever agreed on anything.

But of all things to finally agree on, why does it have to be getting rid of Grandpa's treasures?

And that name: Throop. It's very familiar, someone Grandpa talked about a while ago but I can't remember what he said. My knees start to burn from being so cramped in the corner, but I remain still.

"Before we do anything, I'd like the chance to at least go through everything and let the family choose what they want," Dad says. "My girls, your boys, they're all entitled."

"You heard what Throop said earlier," Uncle Randy says. "I hate to say it but he's right. We don't have time to go through all of it. We need to clean this place out as fast as possible."

I stand up to run back to the kitchen to tell Frankie and instead run smack into Peter. The glass ball drops to the floor with a loud *clunk*.

"Peter! Why are you sneaking around?" I yell. "You almost made me break that!"

"Your mom wants to know if you want any dessert."

"There are so many more important things than dessert!" I pick up the ball and rest it on a small table where my parents put their keys. I push past him and hear him say, "Does that mean I can have it?"

When I get back in the kitchen, I make an announcement: "Frankie. Jolene. Attic. Now."

Jolene jumps off her stool and salutes me.

"Savannah," my mother says. "First of all, tone of voice?"

"Sorry."

"Second of all, to make things go faster, how about you help us wrap up the rest of the food and do the dishes since none of you were here to help set up? Then you and your sisters can go play."

This is precisely why I never hang out in the kitchen.

From the Crow's Nest

After the kitchen is clean enough for the queen of England, we finally escape to the attic, alone. This is our room to arrange how we want. Like the rest of the house, it's full of Grandpa's things, but up here it's more like couches and lamps and old wooden chests, all the furniture that was moved to make room for the more interesting treasures downstairs. A couple of years ago, Grandpa helped us clear out the middle of the room, and we laid down a colorful braided rug. Then Grandpa pulled over a couch and little table that Jolene uses to color on, or that we play games on.

This is where we developed our plan to bomb Peter from the second story with water balloons after he told on me and Frankie for taking the kayak too far into the bay. And where we spy on our neighbor, Ms. Carolina Davis, who we're convinced is a famous celebrity in disguise because she always wears gigantic sunglasses even when it's raining. Every now and then Grandpa would peek his head up into the attic and say, "How are you scallywags doing in the crow's nest?" The "crow's nest" is the lookout on a pirate ship. It makes me sad to think no one will be checking in on us anymore. We have to sail our ship alone now.

I tell my sisters what I overheard in the foyer about Uncle Randy wanting to sell Grandpa's treasures. "We can't let it happen," I say, clinging to my backpack. "These things belong to *our* family. And Grandpa entrusted the map to us, to carry on his search for Blackbeard's treasure."

Frankie looks more worried than I thought she would. "I want to know *why* it's happening," she says. "Mom and Dad love Grandpa's things. They'd never choose to sell them unless something was wrong."

"What could be wrong?"

Frankie shrugs. "I have no idea."

"I told you, I heard Uncle Randy talking to that man in the green hat about it at the church," Jolene says.

"No, you didn't," I say.

"Yes, I did. I'm telling the truth! Before we left. Something about partners in a hairy dance."

"Jolene, you are so strange sometimes," I say.

"Am not."

"Are."

"Am not!"

"You two stop it." Frankie pushes our faces away

from each other. "Maybe that man in the green hat is Throop?"

"I bet you're right!" Suddenly the memory is clear. "Remember that day Grandpa took us to the museum in Beaufort to donate artifacts?"

"No." Jolene shakes her head earnestly.

"It was a long time ago," Frankie says. "You didn't go, you were too little. But yes, I remember. Why?"

"He said something that day about how Throop was the reason Grandpa had to donate those artifacts to the museum. I just can't remember what or why."

"I don't remember that," Frankie says.

"Well, no matter what the reason is, they want to sell everything now. And we can't let it happen. We're going to have to hide it all."

Frankie leans back against the couch. "Unless you have some kind of invisibility power that we don't know about, that wouldn't even be possible." She twirls a long section from the underside of her hair. She always does that when she's thinking. Once, she was thinking so hard she made a giant knot that Mom had to cut out of her hair, and she had a bald patch on her head for months.

"We have to stop them," I say.

"I agree," Frankie says, "but we also need to find out why they want money so bad. And since you are the best sneak, Sav, I enlist you to figure it out."

"I can listen through the grate in the floor when Mom and Dad go to bed."

"Or try to catch them when they're having their coffee before we get up for school," Frankie says.

Jolene sits up straight. "Or just ask them!"

Frankie puts her arm around Jolene. "There're a few things you haven't learned yet. If Mom and Dad wanted us to know something, they'd have told us already."

"Exactly," I say. "Something's going on."

"A constancy," Jolene whispers.

"I think you mean 'a conspiracy,'" Frankie says.

"That's what I said." Jolene nods.

"In the meantime . . ." I lean into my sisters and slide an old wooden board out from under the couch. Grandpa covered it with a star chart, something sailors once used to navigate the seas. We call it our Star Board. "We could ask Blackbeard for help."

Jolene looks unconvinced. She's not a big fan of the Star Board.

"Help us do what?" Frankie asks.

"Find his treasure once and for all," I say.

"What good is that going to do?"

"Because if we find Blackbeard's treasure, we prove that it's real and that Grandpa was right all along. Then no one is going to want to get rid of or sell anything of his ever again."

"They'd probably want to put it all in a museum in New York City," Frankie says, her face lighting up when she realizes the genius of my plan.

"Better yet, they'd probably create a whole museum

here about Grandpa!" I say, and spread my hands out like I'm holding a banner. "The Cornelius Franklin Dare Museum of Pirate History."

"And nobody will laugh at him anymore?" Jolene says, her little eyebrows troubled.

"Exactly," I say. "Now let's do this."

Ghosts in the Rafters

One of the cedar chests in the attic is full of pirate clothes Grandpa collected for us. Some of it's too big, but Grandpa said he did that on purpose so that we'd always have proper attire as we were growing up on his ship. I put on purple-and-black-striped pants with suspenders and a white buttoned-up shirt. Frankie wears a poufed-sleeve shirt and a huge pair of brown buckled pants that are so baggy they look like an old-fashioned skirt. She has a big feathered hat in her hand that she usually wears but this time she tosses it back in the chest. Jolene puts on her favorite thing—a cloth eye patch—but then she sits near the cedar chest and frowns.

"What's the matter with you?" I ask.

"Grandpa never got me a pirate princess dress."

"Aye, that's because dere's no such thing as pirate princesses, matey. They're all queens," I tease her, trying to make her laugh, but she frowns harder. I'm pretty sure it's not the dress that's making her sad. I hope she doesn't start crying. I can't handle crying.

"Wear what you're wearing, then," Frankie says as she lights a few candles around the room. "You don't have to dress like a pirate if you don't want to."

I give Frankie a look.

"What now?" Frankie raises her hands.

"It works better if we're all in character." I try to hand her the feathered hat.

"Sav, just set up the Star Board."

"Grandpa loved when you wore this hat."

"Fine." She puts it on but doesn't look happy about it.

I set the Star Board in the middle of the rug and place the wooden paddle on top. Grandpa said he found the old board on a ship and then he made this flat paddle that has little legs and a small hole in the top to look through. It's like a Ouija board, to contact ghosts, only instead of an alphabet across the board, it's star constellations, and each one stands for a letter. But I am the one who took the time to memorize all the names of the constellations, so only I can interpret the messages.

With stars as the code, he said, if it ever works, I'll know it's legit pirates talking to us. Or at least dead sailors. Across the top he painted THE LONGEST LIVER SHALL HAVE ALL!, which is part of a quote from Blackbeard about who would find his buried treasure. And it has nothing to do with the length of your liver, which Jolene is still trying to get straight. I could tell her it just means whoever lives the longest, but she'll figure it out. It's always more fun to figure things out on your own than to be told the answers all the time.

We all have to gently put our fingers on the paddle and ask Blackbeard a question. If his spirit is in the attic, he'll maybe answer our question. Grandpa often said Blackbeard's ghost liked to swing from the rafters when the house was creaking in a storm. But we have to be serious and really believe he's here. We've only tried this a few times because honestly, even though Grandpa meant it just for fun, it is a little creepy. Although the only thing that's happened was when Jolene knocked over a glass of water that shattered and made us all scream. And that scared the dog and sent her out of the crow's nest with her tail between her legs. Now whenever the board is out, Py leaves the room immediately.

We've also never had a real question to ask Blackbeard. It's always been silly stuff like if Frankie would get an A on her math test and when would Jolene's tooth fall out.

Now everything feels much more important.

I remind my sisters of all the rules. Frankie rolls her eyes. Jolene shivers. We place our fingers on the paddle and I do the talking. Because I always do the talking.

"Dear Edward Teach," I say, using Blackbeard's real name so he knows we are friendly and smart.

"You don't have to say 'dear,'" Frankie says. "You're not writing a letter."

I tell her to close her eyes and shut up.

I start over. "Edward, if you're here, we really need your help this time."

Jolene echoes me, "Yes, Mr. Edward, we really, really, really need your help."

I almost tell her to be quiet too, but she's actually kind of cute and not bossy like Frankie. So I keep going. "Edward, our grandfather, your greatest fan, died on Wednesday and left us, his three favorite grandchildren . . ."

"You don't know that," Frankie says.

I open my eyes and look at her. "Yes, I do."

She doesn't argue and closes her eyes again so I can continue. "He left us the map he's been using his whole life to look for your treasure. It's a map of the island, and he made it himself based on his years of pirate research and treasure hunting. And we already know he was looking somewhere at Springer's Point, so we . . ."

The portal window across the room rattles. We all jump. It rattles even harder. Like someone's shaking it, trying to get out.

Or in.

"Batten down the hatches!" Jolene yells, and ducks as if something is sailing over her head.

"Tell him we don't want to steal it!" Frankie hisses at me. "We just want to keep it safe!"

"I'm trying to! Stop interrupting me!" But I don't get a chance to say anything.

The window rattles so hard in its frame that it suddenly pops open and slams against the wall. Wind rushes into the room. The lamp on the table blinks out.

We all scream and jump ship.

Dad meets us at the bottom of the attic stairs where we run into him and scream again. "What in the world is going on?" He stops us from all falling into a pile in the hallway.

"Nothing," Frankie says, catching her breath first. "We were playing and it freaked out Jolene."

"It sounded like you freaked out the entire neighborhood. I was coming to get you so you can say goodbye to your cousins. They want to leave before the storm picks up too much."

I look at Frankie and she says, "It was only the wind."

Dad ushers us down the hall. "What was only the wind?"

"Nothing," we say.

"All right, then, come on. We're having a quick family meeting in the living room."

Frankie takes off her feathered hat.

Family meetings are never good.

Saying Goodbye

"We already know you're selling all Grandpa's treasures."
I flop onto the couch and cross my arms around a pillow
against my chest. A roll of thunder in the distance times
itself perfectly with my mood. Uncle Randy, Aunt Della,
and Peter are all at the dining table and look quite surprised by my declaration. Little Will is sacked out on the
couch with chocolate all over his face from the dessert I
missed.

"Easy," Mom says, putting a hand on my thigh. "How
do you know this, Savvy?"

"She was sneaking around following our dads," Peter
says.

"You can't sneak in your own house," I say.

"All right, you two," Uncle Randy says. "Can you
chill out for one night?" But he only looks at me.

"I would if Peter wasn't always trying to get me in trouble," I say.

"I'm not! I was just telling the truth," Peter says. He doesn't get it. Peter's like a truth serum. He can't help it. I sigh and apologize.

"All right, thank you, Savvy. Anyway," Dad says. "Yes, you're right. We have a lot of expenses with this old place and it's become overrun with Grandpa's finds anyway. We'd like you kids to all pick out something you'd like to keep to remember Grandpa. There will be more opportunities to do this later, but we thought it might be nice to begin tonight."

My brain starts running through all the things in the house. How could I pick just one? And how can I pick anything at all? Everything should stay exactly where it is. It feels like Grandpa is still here, with all his treasures around us every day. I don't want anything to change. My ears heat up.

"What about Robbie?" Frankie asks. "He's the oldest of all of us. Shouldn't he get to choose something?"

"He didn't want anything," Uncle Randy says. "So it's you girls and Peter, and we'll pick something out for Will." Frankie and I look at each other. Of all the cousins, Robbie spent the least time with Grandpa, but it's surprising he wouldn't want something to remember him by.

"Is there anything that you can think of immediately,

maybe a book or figure that would mean a lot for you to have?" Mom asks us. We all look at each other, no one brave enough to speak first. Or maybe none of us has any idea where to start. Outside the rain has started tapping on the metal roof and the noise fills the silence in the living room. I start hiccupping, because that's what happens when I'm trying not to cry.

Peter takes a big breath and talks fast. "I remember how Grandpa used to walk all over the island and how he'd take some of us almost every single time. He always carried that carved walking stick and I used to try to read what's on it when we'd stop and sit on a bench at the harbor. He'd joke it was in an unknown language and that he found it on a deserted island in the Caribbean. I'd really like that carved walking stick." He lets the rest of his breath out in a big burst of air. "I mean, if that's okay."

"Of course that's okay, Peter," Dad says. "That is a wonderful memory." He gets up and heads out to the hall. I look at the floor and follow a swirly pattern in the rug so I don't have to think too much about Grandpa's walking stick leaving the house. Dad retrieves it and gingerly places it in Peter's hands.

"Girls?" Dad looks at us. His eyes are shiny with tears.

"Are you sure, Dad?" Frankie asks.

"This would make your grandfather so happy," Dad says. "I'm sure."

Within a few minutes, Frankie chooses a leather satchel Grandpa carried his notebook and pen in. "He used to put seashells in this pocket and he'd have peppermints in this one," she says, and lifts a pocket. Sure enough, there are still two candies in there. "I could use it as a new book bag?"

"I love that idea," Mom says.

Jolene chooses a little wooden box carved with flowers and filled with sea glass and tiny misshapen pearls. "His treasure box!" Jolene announces. "I'll keep it safe forever."

No one has the heart to tell her sea glass and the tiny pearls, although pretty, aren't worth anything. I guess to her they are and that's all that matters.

Uncle Randy and Aunt Della pick out an old North Carolina state flag from one of Grandpa's boats over the years to hang up in Will's bedroom, and even an old oil lamp for Robbie, "Just in case he changes his mind someday," Aunt Della says.

And then I'm the only one left.

"There's no way for me to decide." I nearly choke on the words. As each item was given away, it made me wish I'd chosen it, even though they seemed perfect for each person and everyone deserves to have something special. My eyes burn, but I refuse to cry. "I want to keep it all."

"We'll find perfect homes for everything, but you need to decide what's perfect for you first." Mom hugs me tight. "You can have some time, Savvy. You don't have to decide right this second if you're unsure."

I nod.

"All right, we really need to get this little man to bed," Aunt Della says, scooping up Will, who's so sound asleep he doesn't even move. "Thank you, Jack, Anne." She hugs my parents. "Sad as it is, this whole day has been lovely." She passes Will to Uncle Randy and they all say goodbye. Peter seems proud to use the walking stick as he leaves. Mom shuts the door, and except for the rain on the roof, the house is quiet again.

Like nothing ever happened.

Even though it's the worst thing that's ever happened to me.

Frankie kisses our parents and goes upstairs to take a shower, and Mom and Dad put Jolene to bed, leaving me in the living room squeezing a pillow and wondering what in the world I will choose to always remember my grandpa by.

His ivory pipe he used to smoke cherry tobacco with when he was younger?

The bubbly glass balls I've always loved?

A rusty, barnacle-covered compass?

Nothing seems quite right. I'm still sitting on the couch when Dad comes back down.

"Can't decide, Savvy?" He sits and puts his arm around me. I lean into his warm side. We sit like that for a couple of minutes until he says, "I think I have just the thing." He pops up, leaves the room, and comes back with a small box. He hands it to me.

Inside is a thick gold ring I've never seen before. It has etchings on the sides similar to a compass.

"Grandpa gave this to me when I was a little older than you. When I first learned how to sail. Watch this." Dad takes the ring out of the box and somehow slides it so that inner rings unfold from the main ring until it looks like a tiny sphere. Each ring has writing and symbols on it.

"Whoa!" I roll the little sphere in my hand. It's about the size of a grape. "What does all this mean?"

"Each ring is a line in the sky that goes around the entire globe—Tropic of Cancer, Tropic of Capricorn, maybe? I don't remember the rest. Grandpa told me way back then that it was sort of a map of the sky and a tool for navigating the sea. It's called a celestial ring."

I gently close all the rings so they fold back into one ring. "You can't even tell it holds so many secrets."

"Nope."

"I love it." I try it on my fingers, but it's too big for any of them.

"I thought you might." He smiles. "I'll get you a chain and you can wear it as a necklace. Sound good?"

"Thanks, Dad." I nod and hug him tight. "You're sure you don't want to keep it?"

"I've had it long enough. It's yours now. But it's time to get ready for bed."

"Okay."

I pass Frankie in the hall on the way to my room and whisper, "We start looking for clues tomorrow."

"Aye aye," she says, and before she disappears into her room, I tell her, "Grandpa's bag looks great on you."

I lie in my bed opening and closing the celestial ring. It's not the first night without Grandpa in the house, but somehow it feels like he's farther away now and might drift a little more every day, like a boat without an anchor. "Don't worry, Grandpa," I whisper into the dark. "I won't let anyone forget you."

The Cord of Three

The end of summer is like a long sigh. Everything starts to calm down in town. The village is clearing out. Vacationers wrapping up their holidays, fewer boats on the water, less noise. You can feel the salty air starting to change too; autumn's crisper skies and cooler nights aren't long off. Some trees are starting to lose their leaves, tumbling to the ground like tears. But it's still hot, really hot, even at nine in the morning. And the Queen Mary is a sad place to be right now. Leaving the house feels good.

The three of us run down the front steps and grab our skateboards and helmets from the shed out back. Ms. Carolina Davis is also out back watering flowers in her yard and she watches us from behind her glasses.

"Morning, Ms. Davis," Jolene says, and waves.

"Morning to you too, doll face." Ms. Davis waves

back. The rhinestones in her glasses sparkle around her eyes like little stars.

"Do you think she sleeps with them on?" I whisper to Frankie, who says nothing but shoves my shoulder. "What? She can't hear me."

"You have such a big mouth."

"Better than having a big butt!" I tease.

Frankie looms over me, and she's so tall I can see up her nose.

"Sorry."

"Uh-huh," she says, and hands me my board. "Everyone on deck. Rope up."

Frankie leads the way, pushing off on her skateboard in front of me. She has a rope tied to her waist like a belt so that her hands are free. The other end trails behind her and leads to my board. I wrap the rope around my hand and help push off. Behind me, Jolene holds the very end of the rope and sits on her board, and we pull her through town. She has the bag with Grandpa's map wrapped in one arm and grips the rope with the other. She hums a tune I recognize well, something Grandpa always whistled about pirates and rum.

Treasure hunting was Grandpa's hobby but he also made many maps in his life, and this one is unlike any other. The first time he showed it to me, he said, "There's a secret in this map, Savvy."

I ran my hand over the crinkly paper. "What kind of secret?"

"The kind that can change your life, if you let it."

"Will it make me rich?"

"In some ways, I suppose." Grandpa smiled. "Maps have a way of giving you what you need at just the right time."

I need it to have the secret to save everything aboard the Queen Mary, everything we've ever loved and known.

"Grandpa left us the map so we could finish his search, prove he was right all along," I say, thinking about his hand-drawn lines of Ocracoke Island and how delicate and fancy his handwriting was. "Grandpa will be super famous after we find the treasure."

"I'm going to trust you on this one," Frankie says, "because we have no other options."

"Yeah." Jolene sighs. "We're despicable."

"I think you mean 'desperate,'" Frankie says as she pushes off the sandy pavement with extra force to get us across an intersection. I help a little bit by leaning forward and to the left as she makes the turn.

"That's what I said." Jolene adjusts her eye patch. She's been wearing it since yesterday and I'm pretty sure she's never taking it off again.

We pass Mr. Brown, the librarian and one of our teachers from school, who shakes his head every time he sees us. Frankie does most of the work to pull us through the village, but she doesn't mind. She's tall for her age and strong, and only *I* know this, but she's been hanging out with a boy named Ryan who's fifteen and has taught her how to surf. She says she wanted to prove she could do it. But I think she just wants to hang out with him.

In the center of town, we go around Silver Lake, the inlet from the bay that has a harbor and little shops and restaurants around it. Morning near the water is all clanking masts and screaming seagulls competing for scraps of fish thrown overboard. Pelicans wait at the end of the docks and dive in when they see fishermen throwing leftovers into the water. And there are tons of out-of-towners zipping around on bikes, talking very fast and loud. Near our house, things are much quieter, but here there's always someone to watch and eavesdrop on, at least during half the year. After September, when most of the Northerners go home, the island becomes much quieter.

Uncle Randy's boat is docked and we wave to him as we pass.

"Morning, girls! There're still a lot of vacationers in town. Make sure you pay attention on the road!"

"We will," Frankie shouts back. She skates harder, nearly losing both me and Jolene. But I keep my balance and Jolene holds on tight; we're used to Frankie's skating. And we're used to Uncle Randy thinking our parents shouldn't let us run around all over town, so it's all good.

A car with New Jersey plates passes us and then slows down. When we catch up, a lady leans her head out the window and says, "Look at you three, aren't you inventive! Look at them, Dan, like three little nesting dolls, exact copies of each other in different sizes. Three little Southern belles!"

I don't have any idea what she's talking about; we don't look anything alike, but we all smile and glance at each other because she sounds like she's pinching her nose when she talks and there's too many "W's" in her words.

Before the lady and the Dan guy pull away, she tells Frankie we better be careful going down the road like that. "Even though you're tall as a sycamore, your sisters are hard to see on those skateboards."

Frankie says, "Yes, ma'am," but when the car pulls away, she mumbles, "Mind your own beeswax, dingbatter." Jolene and I laugh out loud. Grandpa used to say "dingbatter" all the time. Vacationers are a way of life in the village, at least in the summer, and as Uncle Randy says, we need them, but that doesn't mean we want all of them. Although Uncle Randy *really* needs them, since his whole job is to take people out on deep-sea fishing trips.

"What did she call you, Frankie?" Jolene asks.

"A big tree," Frankie grumbles.

Jolene giggles nonstop the rest of the way. "Frankie's a big tree."

The historical society is like a little museum and library in one. It has a lot of Grandpa's published articles and artifacts on display, so first thing Sunday morning, that's where we go looking for clues. We know after Grandpa stopped searching for shipwrecks, he spent many hours with a special detector hunting for gold coins at Springer's Point before he died, so we're thinking that's the best place to start. Hopefully between the map he left us and the stuff at the museum, we can find something more about what he knew and found.

Mrs. Taylor runs the museum, and when we get there, she gives us an enormous hug. She's been a friend of our family's for many years. Although so has almost everyone else.

"Oh, my sweet little girls," she says. "I'm so sorry about your grandpa. I wanted to come to the services yesterday but I had to help my daughter with the new baby and all, and . . ."

"It's okay, Mrs. Taylor," Frankie says. "We know you loved Grandpa."

Mrs. Taylor looks like she might melt on the floor. "I did, so. What can I do for you, loves?"

"We'd like to be near Grandpa's things, if that's okay?" I ask.

"You know you're always welcome." She happily gestures toward the room with Grandpa's papers and special findings. She disappears for a moment and then returns with a large envelope.

"I didn't think you'd be by so soon after," she says.

"But I have a special package for you." She hands the envelope to Frankie. I lean over and Jolene stands on tiptoe to see. Our names are on the front with *Do not open until September 1996* in Grandpa's handwriting. I look up at Mrs. Taylor, but don't even have to ask.

"Whatever is in there, he specifically asked me to hold on to it for you girls." She smiles and leaves the room.

We were here all the time with Grandpa, and sometimes I volunteer to help Mrs. Taylor with special events and ghost tours in the village, which is why I'm pretty sure she'd hire me if I ever needed a job, even though I'm four years too young to have a job. She was a good friend to Grandpa for a very long time.

But this is unexpected.

"Open it, Frankie!" Jolene says, bouncing on her toes so she can see. We all sit down among the glass display cases and Frankie carefully tears the envelope open. Inside is a single piece of paper with a coded message:

```
OWXRY, BWJRY, INBR, NOG EIBR

NXWJOG RYI QBSNOG NENQRB N HJIBR.

YQGGIO RWWSB NOG KSJIB NXI ZWJOG,

MQXNRI RXINBJXI RYXWJPYWJR AWJX RWEO.

XQGGSIB NOG MJTTSIB AWJ'FI NSENAB VOWEO;

BRWXQIB Q'FI RWSG AWJ NB AWJ'FI PXWEO.
```

```
BRNXR EQRY RYI UNM NOG RXJBR AWJX AWJRY,

BWUIRQUIB RYI WCFQWJB QB RYI RXJRY.

NOG XIUIUCIX EYNR Q'FI BNQG WZ RYII:

BRXIOPRY RWPIRYIX, N KWXG WZ RYXII.

EYIO QO GWJCR, MSINBI XIUIUCIX:

Q'U EQRY AWJ NSENAB NOG ZWXIFIX.
```

Jolene squishes up her nose and eyes. "What does *that* say?"

"'Owxry, bwjry . . . nog . . .'" Frankie reads the words just the way they look on the paper.

Jolene laughs. "You made up a new language!"

I take the paper away. "It's not a language," I whisper. "It's a cryptogram."

"How can you tell?" Frankie asks.

"Because Grandpa made these all the time for me. And you can buy books of them at the big market in Hatteras in the checkout line. I do them when I'm waiting for the lady to ring Mom up. Each letter just stands for another letter."

I pull a pencil out of my backpack and try a couple of combinations. It can take a little while to figure out what the letters are supposed to be, but if you look for patterns it helps reveal the true words. Punctuation helps too.

"Look," I show Frankie. "This word 'NOG' shows up a lot and then there is an 'N' all by itself, so I know 'N' is either 'A' or 'I' so I'll start with 'A' . . ."

"Ugh, Sav, you're killing me," Frankie says. "You lost me at 'NOG.'"

"I can do it." I start decoding the letters. Frankie never has patience for puzzles. I was the only one who'd ever sit with Grandpa and try to figure them out. Which makes me pause for a minute and wonder if he was making me practice for this reason. Maybe he knew someday he'd have to give me a very important code to crack.

"What?" Frankie asks. "Why'd you stop?"

"Nothing," I say, and get back to work.

After a few minutes, and only a couple of mistakes, I finally have it.

I read it out loud to my sisters:

North, South, East, and West
Around the island awaits a quest.
Hidden tools and clues are found,
Pirate treasure throughout your town.
Riddles and puzzles you've always known;
Stories I've told you as you've grown.

Start with the map and trust your youth,
Sometimes the obvious is the truth.
And remember what I've said of thee:
Strength together, a cord of three.
When in doubt, please remember:
I'm with you always and forever.

We're quiet for a few minutes looking at Grandpa's loopy coded letters, the words he left for us. Frankie sighs. Jolene sniffles a little bit.

"I told you," I whisper. "He had some kind of plan all along."

"So where is it all hidden?" Frankie asks, taking the letter and flipping it over like there might be more information on the back. "That can't be it!"

"He wouldn't put the answers in the poem," I said. "He obviously meant it only for us to figure out. Just like he said, 'Start with the map.'"

"But why?" Frankie asks. "Why make us go to all this trouble with these frustrating clues? Why not just leave us a letter or something to tell us what we're looking for?"

"Maybe he was afraid someone else would find it first," Jolene says.

We look at each other and it's like a light bulb pops on for each one of us at the same exact time. I can't believe I didn't see it earlier.

The man in the green hat.

Throop.

"He's trying to get all Grandpa's things out of the house so *he* can find this map and get the treasure," I whisper.

"How would he know about it?" Frankie asks.

"Remember I just told you yesterday they used to work together?"

Frankie shakes her head a little bit. "This all seems kind of strange, but let's look."

We spread the map out on the floor in a corner of the room. Frankie gently places a foggy glass bottle on one side and I put a metal bowl from one of the cases on the other to hold the corners down. My favorite thing in the case is a little metal tool with a strong magnifying glass that was once used to read maps. You slide it over the paper and look down through it to read any tiny words. We have a regular magnifying glass at home, but there's something cool about using one that was found in a real shipwreck.

Jolene gently pages through a captain's log while Frankie and I examine the map. The log's written in English but the handwriting is long and scrawling and every "F" looks like an "S" so it's pretty confusing, but she always likes to look through it. Frankie holds on to the sextant, an old-fashioned tool sailors used for navigating the sea before computers. All of these artifacts help us feel closer to Grandpa. If only they could talk and tell us the secrets he knew. We've looked at this map a million times in the last few days and it still looks like a regular map of Ocracoke.

Sometimes the obvious is the truth.

"Oh, excuse me, lassies," a man with a deep voice says as he comes into the room. We all look up and I know exactly what I'm going to see before I see it: the green hat with the yellow anchor. My sisters and I all freeze.

He's very tall and has large, dark eyebrows that almost touch in the middle and a dark mole on his cheek. "I didn't realize anyone else liked to study in this room. I'll come back later." He tips his hat at us and backs out again, but not before his eyes find the map.

"Throop," Frankie says without making a sound. I nod. Has to be.

Jolene whispers, "He's definitely the one who was talking to Uncle Randy about the hairy dance."

"Are you totally sure?" I ask.

"I remember his hat."

"Plenty of people wear green hats. You have to be positive." I'm pretty sure I'd remember a hat on such a big man at a funeral, especially since most people don't wear hats at funerals. Then again, I spent most of my time looking for a way to sneak out of the church.

"I'm positive," Jolene says.

"Do you think he's following us?" I ask Frankie.

"Could be. Or maybe he just came here for the same reason we did—to look at Grandpa's things for clues."

"Let's hurry up." I slide the magnifier over Grandpa's map looking for any interesting marks or symbols. Mostly it's street names and basic locations like Springer's Point Preserve and the lighthouse, the old war cemetery, and Silver Lake, all places we skate past every day. Grandpa even added the Queen Mary and our school, which makes me groan just thinking about going back tomorrow. School only started a couple of weeks ago, but it was a lot of the same stuff we learned last year and is always the same kids. Thanksgiving break can't come soon enough. I'd much rather be treasure hunting than doing fractions.

But I can't find anything that stands out until I sit up and accidently run the magnifier over the word "Ocracoke."

"Oh!"

"What is it?" Frankie asks.

"I don't know yet, but I think I found something." I turn the map and show her with the magnifier. Inside each letter of our town name is a light, swirly pattern. At first it seems like a wispy spiderweb design. But at a closer look, you can see that it's actually teeny-tiny letters inside the letters that make up the word "Ocracoke."

Grandpa left us another code.

One-Eyed Wonder

"Is it the same as the poem?" Frankie asks. I shake my head. It seems like completely random letters. But knowing Grandpa, it's definitely not random.

"We have to take this home," Frankie whispers. "It's going to take us forever to figure out what all those letters are for and we can't risk him walking in again and seeing what we're doing."

"Let's go back Springer's Point," I say. "We know Grandpa was always looking for stuff there anyway. We'll figure out what the letters say and find the treasure right away!"

"Good plan," Frankie says, and I can't help but smile because she thinks I have a good idea. "You and Jolene go to the park. I'm going to run home and get us water and snacks."

"And shovels."

"I don't think it's going to be that easy, Sav."

"Just in case!"

I gently roll up the map and put it in my backpack and we put everything else away exactly how we found it. I want to take the magnifier with us, but Frankie says she'll bring ours instead, so I put it back in the case. We say goodbye to Mrs. Taylor and she says, "I hope you found what you were looking for!"

"And then some!" Jolene says, grinning wildly, and we shush her and have to push her out the door. Frankie races home and Jolene and I head to the park.

With one foot on my board, I use the other to push off the sandy street, pulling Jolene along.

"You really need to learn how to ride that thing yourself," I tell her.

"Why?" she asks. "You and Frankie always pull me."

I don't even bother arguing with her, even though pulling her makes me sweat like a bottle of soda pop on a hot summer night. On the way we pass Kate and LouAnn on their bikes. Up until last year that would have been me with Kate, not LouAnn. I try to get past them quickly. "Sorry about your grandpa," one of them says. I think it's Kate, but I can't be sure because I pick up speed as quickly as I can to get Jolene away from them. I'm not as fast as Frankie though.

"Thanks!" Jolene shouts back.

"Don't talk to them."

"Why?"

"Because we're not friends anymore."

"But they were nice."

I don't know what to say to that because she's right. But they weren't so nice last year when I brought a globe to school and tried to quiz the class on different countries. They only called me weird.

"It's because you're interested in things they don't understand, Savvy," Grandpa told me. "Instead of trying to understand, calling you weird is the easiest way for them to explain it to themselves."

"I'm not weird," I said.

"Of course you are!" He crossed his eyes at me and stuck his tongue out. "All the best people are weird."

"Grandpa!" I scolded him, but he made me laugh, which I guess was the point.

"You're in a very small school, Savvy. Give it time, let everyone grow up a little bit. It'll get better."

Maybe Grandpa was right, maybe Kate felt bad now, because I sure did. But either way it was easier to stay away from most of the kids at school.

Besides, other than Frankie and Jolene, Grandpa was the only friend I needed.

The hiccups start and I have to stop myself and focus on skating so I don't crash poor Jolene into a tree.

"Are you okay?" Jolene asks me.

"Everything's fine." I skate harder than ever. I think I might be almost as fast as Frankie.

Fortunately it's only a couple of turns till we get

to the park, and we're there in no time, so I can forget about all of that. I roll to the beginning of the trail and pop up my board, and we set mine and Jolene's to the side. Silently we sit down and take off our shoes, tossing them over with our boards. Walking through the park barefoot is so much nicer than with sneakers. As we're about to head down the sandy trail, we hear the sound of tires and a familiar voice behind us. I don't even have to turn to know it's Peter.

Grandpa's walking stick is strapped along the side of Peter's bike and his hair is a mess as usual. "What are y'all doing out here?"

"We're meeting the president for lunch," I say sarcastically. "What do you think we're doing? We're"—and suddenly I can't think of anything good to make up—"going to the beach."

"Can I come?"

"Nope," Jolene says before I can even make up a good reason to say no.

"Why are you wearing that?" he asks, pointing to Jolene's eye patch. She crosses her arms, but doesn't answer.

"Whatever, one-eyed wonder," Peter says.

Jolene grins. Nothing ever bothers that kid. Sometimes I wish I could be like that.

Peter looks at me for an answer and I don't say anything either. I feel kind of bad that we always tell him no, but since that's what we always say, he doesn't seem to suspect anything. And I'm not sure Grandpa wanted Peter to know about the map, so it seems better this way.

"You're probably doing something boring anyway, like memorizing the periodic table." He swings his bike around and shouts, "I'm going to go find Colin. He's way more fun than you anyway!" Little does he know I already have the periodic table memorized. My dad gave me a chart from his classroom last year and it hangs over my bed.

As Peter rides away, Frankie comes down the road on her board. She's wearing a backpack and has two shovels propped on her shoulder as she weaves down the street. I'm pretty sure she can do anything on her board. She nods to Peter, but he ignores her. When she gets to us, she's grinning.

"I'm assuming you chased him away," she says, handing me a shovel and laughing.

"Jolene did it," I said. "I didn't have to say a word. Her eye patch scared him off."

"Nice work." Frankie holds up a hand and Jolene gives her a high five. "Now let's go find a shady corner to start. Preferably with no ants."

There are a couple of picnic tables throughout the park, so we pick one deep in the oak trees off the path a little bit so that no one will walk by and see what we're doing. Also so we can be in the shade, because yesterday the sun fried us like fritters. The table is clean and even though a little brown lizard scurries across the top, it's mostly ant-free, so Frankie reluctantly agrees. She's brought back notebooks and the magnifying glass. We spread out the map and get to work.

"You use this, Sav." She hands me the glass. "And I'll transcribe."

"What does that mean?" Jolene asks.

"That means I'll write down every letter Sav reads out loud."

"What am I going to do?" Jolene asks.

"You're the lookout," I say. "The most important job on the ship. You have to alert us if any other pirates are nearby."

She salutes me, looks around, and decides to climb up in the tree branches above us. "I can see best from up here!"

"Perfect," Frankie says. "Go ahead, Sav, I'm ready when you are."

I use the magnifying glass to figure out every single letter written inside the word "Ocracoke." I call them out to Frankie one letter at a time and she groups them together. Her notes look like alphabet soup.

O: QKXXEZT

C: EIAVLLR

R: KROFVL

A: DAQEFKXEO

C: KQYLRQ

O: FVORKL
K: BLVICQRO
E: YIBTQIBCL

"Grandpa," I say under my breath to myself.

"What is it?" Frankie asks.

"This is a lot more complicated than the poem."

I'm good at unscrambling words and solving puzzles, but there are so many letters and no patterns or punctuation.

"What in the world do we do with these now?" Frankie asks, turning her notebook at different angles, as if that will help shake the letters into their proper place. I turn it toward myself to get a better look.

From above, Jolene says, "What's next?"

"I'm thinking," I say, harsher than I mean to sound. I look up at my sister's hurt expression. "Sorry, Jo. Maybe it's an anagram."

"Here we go again," Frankie says. "Remind me what that is?"

"An anagram is just a word scramble."

"This has to be more than one word," Frankie says. "And there are way too many 'X's' and 'Q's'. It doesn't make any sense. You can't make words out of these letters."

I rest my chin in my hand. "Yeah, I know." We're all quiet for a little while, thinking. I try to remember the different codes Grandpa used to give me. "These are like the puzzle books Grandpa had me work on in church so I'd sit still. I think he was preparing me to solve the most important code of all."

"I don't know," Frankie says. "We should ask Dad."

"There's a reason Grandpa left it to us, not Dad."

"We can trust Dad," Frankie says.

"I know. But I want to figure this out myself."

Frankie sighs. She hates not following rules. "It'll be fine," I say.

We both look up at Jolene, who's grinning like the Cheshire cat and says, "Sav's going to save everything aboard the Queen Mary."

I really hope she's right.

All Hands on Deck

As I work on figuring out exactly what kind of code Grandpa left us, Frankie and Jolene offer suggestions. It makes it more confusing though, so I ask them to stop. Then they are so quiet I can't think. Frankie's boy friend—her friend who's a boy, not a boyfriend—walks by with his dog and she runs over to say hi to make sure he doesn't come over to us. She leans against a tree and twirls her hair as Ryan tells her something I can't hear. He'd better not stick around. Jolene jumps out of the tree and joins them, and Ryan holds up a hand so she can slap him five. The three of them talk about something that must be the most hilarious thing Frankie's ever heard.

"I could use some help, you know," I shout over to my sisters. Frankie gives me a look and keeps talking to Ryan. By the time she finally says goodbye, I think I've figured it out anyway. Jolene climbs back up into the tree to reclaim her lookout post and Frankie sits next to me on the bench.

"Do you *like him*, like him?" I ask her.

"Who?" Frankie acts as though she has no idea what I'm talking about, but her face turns bright red.

"You know who. Ryan."

"Don't be ridiculous."

"What were you talking about?"

She and Jolene answer at the same time:

"Mind your own business," Frankie says to me.

"They're going surfing later!" Jolene grins.

Frankie glares at Jolene. "Thanks."

"You can't go surfing later. It's a school night," I say. So much for not breaking rules. I guess she thinks that only applies to me.

"Thanks, Mom junior, I'm aware. Can we just get back to work here?" Frankie pulls the paper closer to herself and pretends to read it.

"You're willing to get in trouble just to hang out with *Ryan*?"

"Savannah. Can you please focus?"

"Jolene knows but you weren't going to tell me?"

Frankie sighs. "Savvy, I'm going surfing with Ryan. There. Are you happy now?"

"Yes." I give her a smug smile. "Sisters should tell each other everything."

"Uh-huh."

"Anyway, I think it *is* a word scramble," I say. "But

sort of like the poem, with letters standing for other letters. But I'm not sure how, yet."

"Why would Grandpa do this to us?" Frankie asks, leaning her chin into her hand. She looks totally bored now, like she'd rather be somewhere else.

"I guess he thought no one else would bother."

"Well, he was right about that," Frankie says. "No one except you, anyway."

"And that green-hat guy," Jolene whispers down to us.

"Exactly. Thank you, Jolene. Now do you want me to unscramble this mess or not?"

"Of course I do. Sorry." Frankie tries to be interested as I arrange and rearrange letters all over the page.

After about three minutes Jolene whines, "I'm hungry. How long is this going to take?"

"It'll take as long as it takes, Jolene," I say, but I'm wondering the same thing myself and am afraid of losing both my sisters' help. I try different letter combinations to make different words, but nothing works. Nothing makes sense.

"Can I see Grandpa's poem again?" I ask Frankie. She hands it over.

> *And remember what I've said of thee:*
> *Strength together, a cord of three.*

"'Cord of three,'" I say, and look at Frankie.
"What about it?"

"That's us, the three of us. He used to say we were stronger when we worked together instead of when we fought, remember?"

"Yes, but I don't get it."

"The number three means something." I tap at the paper. "But I don't know what."

"This is like all those silly riddles he used to say," Jolene says as she hangs upside down from one of the smaller tree branches. "I couldn't ever figure them out either."

I keep trying things but the letters don't make sense. There're too many consonants, not enough vowels, like Frankie said. I think, *What if this code is too hard for me? What if Grandpa was wrong thinking I'm smart enough to crack it?*

Cord of three.

And then I've got it. "Cord of three!" I shout, then lower my voice. "*Code* of three. Grandpa had a code of three. It shifts the alphabet over three letters."

"Huh?" Frankie asks. I love when I know something she doesn't. It doesn't happen very often. But Frankie was never as into puzzles as I was.

"Watch." I write down the entire alphabet and show them how they translate.

A=D
B—E

C=F
D=G
E=H
F=I
G=J
H=K
I=L
J=M
K=N
L=O
M=P
N=Q
O=R
P=S
Q=T
R=U
S=V
T=W
U=X
V=Y
W=Z
X=A
Y=B
Z=C

I figure out all the real letters and write them in new groups.

O: TNAAHCW

C: HLDYOOU

R: NURIYO

A: GDTHINAHR

C: NTBOUT

O: IYRUNO

K: EOYLFTUR

E: BLEWTLEFO

"That's still a jumbled mess," Frankie says.

"I know, but now at least we have the right letters." It takes a lot longer than the poem, but this time Frankie and Jolene help. We try forming all kinds of words, writing down all the combinations we come up with.

"All I get is 'button,'" Frankie says. "I can't do this."

Nothing seems to go together until suddenly I form "left elbow" from the last group of letters.

"Left elbow?" Jolene says. "This is all too confusing."

Frankie starts twirling her hair.

"Stop," I say. "You're going to pull your hair out again. What are you thinking?"

"I'm thinking exactly what Jolene was thinking a little while ago."

"That you're hungry?" Jolene's eyes light up. She's so ready to go home.

"No. About the riddles Grandpa used to tell us. Think, Savvy. Like he says in the poem—stories and puzzles we grew up with."

"Oh!" I say. "ELBOW! Frankie, you're a genius!"

Frankie smiles and shrugs.

"I don't get it!" Jolene says.

"Watch." I arrange all the letters in each group until I have the entire riddle written out on the paper.

What can you hold in your right hand but not in your left? Your left elbow.

"That was the answer to that riddle?" Jolene says. "I can't believe I never figured that out!"

"Yeah, but now what?" I ask, losing all my excitement from before. "'Your left elbow' doesn't make any sense at all. How does the riddle help us find the treasure?"

"I'm not sure yet, but Grandpa knew we'd get this far. He knew you'd be able to figure out the poem and find this code, Sav," Frankie says. "And this clue is clearly only for us because he used to tell us that silly joke all the time. But how it's all connected . . ." Frankie shakes her head. "I just don't know."

"Grandpa wasn't keeping it so easy after all," Jolene says.

"No, he wasn't," I say.

"Grandpa wasn't keeping what so easy?" Peter asks, suddenly appearing next to us with Ryan, Kate, and LouAnn.

"Peter!" I cover the paper I'm working on.

Mortified, Frankie folds over the map and puts her

head down. "This is so embarrassing," she whispers to the table.

When none of us know what else to say, Peter continues, "What's that map of?"

"Jolene!" I yell. She was supposed to be watching for other pirates. Peter is worse than a pirate. And Peter plus Ryan and Kate *and* LouAnn is the ultimate worst!

"None of your beeswax!" Jolene says to Peter. She's flipped herself upright now and has her arms crossed. "I'm sorry I wasn't a good lookout, me hearties," she says to us, her bottom lip starting to stick out.

"It's okay, Jolene," Frankie says, finally looking up from the map. She doesn't make eye contact with anyone except Jolene. I don't understand why she's so embarrassed. "We were all focused on what we were doing. It's not your fault." She gives me the big-sister look of death.

"How's it *my* fault?"

"Savannah, you're exhausting." She starts packing up all our things.

Peter sits on the table right next to me and asks us again what we're doing.

"Boring things," I say.

"Funny," he says. "I was just teasing you. Come on, seriously. What are you doing?"

"I thought you were going to go find Colin," I say.

"He was busy and I found them instead," Peter says.

"We thought we could hang out," Kate says. "Since we're all here and . . ."

"It's not a great time," I say, but half regret it because part of me would like to hang out with Kate if she wants to be friends again. Peter slips the map out from under the other papers and unfolds it.

"Hey!" I scramble up after him, but it's too late.

"What is this?" he asks. The other three look over his shoulder. "This is really cool. Is it one of Grandpa's?"

None of us speak. Frankie still won't look at Ryan. Or anyone, for that matter.

"Come on, guys. Let's head to the beach," Ryan says, shaking his floppy hair. "Frankie, you can join later when you're done. You too, Sav, if you want."

"What about me?" Jolene asks.

I smack her arm and tell her she's too little anyway.

"Oh my gosh, she's so cute with the eye patch," LouAnn says. She and Kate say goodbye and leave back down the trail with Ryan. Frankie looks like she can breathe again and stops shoving things in her backpack.

"I'll be right there," Peter says. After they're out of sight, he asks us again what the map is for.

This time I decide to tell him the truth. It's not like any of our parents would even care if Peter tattle-taled that we were looking at one of Grandpa's maps, especially one that involved Blackbeard, because they don't believe Blackbeard had a treasure. "We're trying to find Blackbeard's buried treasure."

Peter looks at all three of us like he's trying to figure out if we're tricking him again. I guess we do trick him a lot. But when none of us smile, he cracks up laughing. "You're serious?"

"Yes, we're serious," I say. "Grandpa was serious. Why shouldn't we be?"

Still laughing, Peter says, "Because everyone knows there is no treasure. Nothing has ever been found. It's all a fake legend." He jumps down from the table and dusts off his shorts. "Blackbeard was crazy, and, I hate to say it, but so was Grandpa. Don't you know that? Don't your parents tell you anything?"

We look at him blankly. None of us know what to say. Not even me.

"Grandpa. Was not. Crazy." Jolene glares at him with her one eye, serious as ever.

"Yes, he was. At the end. My dad said so. I would never talk bad about him like some others do. Grandpa was always the nicest man, but he had some kind of memory problem. He didn't know the difference between real and make-believe. Especially not in the last few months."

"You're a liar, Peter Dare!" Jolene screams, and jumps out of the tree to chase him down. I grab her by the shoulders and stop her. We all know Peter never lies.

"You better go home," Frankie tells Peter.

"I'm sorry," Peter says, actually looking very sorry now that he's upset Jolene so much. "I thought you knew that. I thought all the cousins knew that. He was a good storyteller, though. I can understand why you thought everything about Blackbeard was true."

"Just go *home*, Peter," Frankie says again. "We don't need you here to make fun."

"I'm not. I promise. I thought you knew," Peter says as he stumbles back from us. "I always say the wrong thing. I'm sorry."

We watch him walk away before any of us says anything. I think my ribs are going to crack with how hard I'm breathing. I sit down at the table and put my head on the map. We knew Grandpa had memory problems, especially this last summer, but Mom and Dad never acted like it was a big deal. They said lots of older people have memory problems.

No one ever said he didn't know the difference between real and make-believe.

"Tell me it's not true, Frankie," I say, hoping she can't hear my voice shaking.

"I don't know," Frankie says.

And that's bad because Frankie might not know codes, but she knows everything else.

Cleaning Out the Captain's Quarters

"Did you have a nice time with Mrs. Taylor?" Mom asks when we come through the door. She's sitting at the dining table sorting piles of old books and notepads. Mom is often organizing things like this because she studies languages and gives talks on stuff like how important the letter "Q" is. When I think about it, maybe that's where I get my superdecoding ability. I'll have to talk to her about that one, but for right now, she must be able to tell we didn't have a nice time because she stops what she's doing and asks if everything is okay. "Frankie? You look angry."

"Everything's fine," Frankie says, and looks at me like she's warning me not to tell Mom what we were doing. Jolene seems uncertain too.

"What's all that?" I ask Mom.

"Oh, just some of Grandpa's notebooks and sketches

from one of the old trunks," she says. She gently sets down the old book in her hand and looks at us with a little frown.

"Are you throwing these away?" I ask, stepping up to the table and lifting a few things. I can see Grandpa's work on everything, diagrams of ships, half-finished maps, pages and pages of his loopy handwriting.

"No, not yet, Savvy. I'm simply organizing. There were three or four trunks filled with paper. I've gotten it down to this. Trying to figure out what's important."

"It's all important!" Jolene says.

"It does seem that way, doesn't it?" Mom says, looking at the huge pile in front of her. Frankie and Jolene each pick a chair next to her as she pages through a leather journal. "These aren't things that people will want to buy, I don't think. I'm not sure how to decide."

"It's easy," I say from across the table. "We keep it all."

Jolene rests her head on Mom's shoulder as Mom talks. "In a perfect world, that's exactly what I would do. I'd keep it for as long as I could, until you girls were old enough to sort through it yourselves. But we don't have that much time, so tough decisions have to be made now."

"Why don't we have time?" I ask.

Mom clears her throat and goes back to sorting. "I only meant the quicker the better."

The portrait of Grandpa is on the wall right behind Mom's head. I keep looking at it, wishing he'd give me one of his funny expressions, or maybe climb right out and tell Mom she's making a huge mistake.

"Mom," Frankie asks, pulling me out of my daydream. "Did Grandpa, um, was he . . . ?" She can't figure out how to ask the question in a polite way.

"Frances wants to know if Grandpa was crazy," I say, crossing my arms.

Mom looks at all three of us, concerned. "Of course not. And I don't like that word. He was, well, he was eccentric, but he most certainly was not crazy."

"What's 'centric'?" Jolene asks.

"It means he was a little weird," Frankie tells her.

"He was not!" I say, slapping my hand on the table. Mom covers it with hers.

"Calm down, loudmouth," Frankie says. "I didn't mean bad weird. I meant different weird. Even Grandpa said he was weird!"

"'Crazy' and 'weird' might not be the best words to use," Mom says, glancing at me. She knows how much I hate it when kids say that to me. "Girls, your grandfather was one of the smartest people I've ever known. And very smart people sometimes look at the world a little bit differently than others, which sometimes makes *other* people think they are weird. Cornelius Franklin Dare was none of those things. He was certainly not crazy. He was kind, gentle, and an amazing storyteller. But you all know this. You lived with your grandfather your entire lives. So what makes you ask that, Frankie?"

Frankie shrugs. "People say stuff."

"Then you let people say stuff," Mom says. "You're named after one of the most amazing people this town has ever known." She rubs Frankie's cheek, which makes my sister smile. I wish I had been given Grandpa's middle name. I'd appreciate it way more than Frankie.

"So, if he wasn't cra . . . what Peter said he was, then he was right," I say. "About stuff like buried treasure."

"Peter said this?" Mom tilts her head a little bit. "Savvy, there's a big difference between what people say and being fanciful. Your grandpa loved to tell you girls ghost stories, and give you puzzles and games to figure out. But that doesn't mean every single thing he told you was true. Does that make sense?"

"But he spent his whole life trying to find Blackbeard's treasure," I say.

"Exactly," Mom says. "And he never found it."

"Because it's still out there!"

Mom sighs. "I don't know that it is, sweetheart. Most shipwrecks and artifacts your grandfather searched for, he found, but not all. His work was often collaborative with other historians, based on logic, science, and history. Until he got swept up in this Blackbeard thing."

"But don't you think if anyone knew the truth it would have been Grandpa?" I ask.

"Almost all experts agree there is no treasure," Mom says. "But your grandpa wouldn't accept that. I don't know if you girls know this, but he gave up his job for it. Left his business partner, decided to move here. And because of his dementia, eventually his memory and ability to make sense of things was not what it used to be, so he was on a quest that was forever changing. I wouldn't take it as far as what Peter told you. Uncle Randy and Aunt Della have different ideas about these matters. Regardless, Grandpa never found anything."

"Blackbeard was *very* crafty," Jolene says.

"Perhaps," Mom says, scratching the top of Jolene's head. "I don't mean to ruin your fun, girls. I know you love and miss your grandpa and this is a wonderful way to keep him close to you. There's no harm in believing in a little magic, but I want you to understand the reality of it all." She looks at the pile and sighs. "I think I'll let your father do this part. I'm going to go start on the closets."

"I'll help," Jolene says, and she takes Mom's hand as they leave the room and head upstairs.

Frankie and I stare at the pile.

"Do you think she knows what we're doing?" I ask Frankie.

"No. She'd have said something about the map if she knew. What are you thinking?"

"I'm thinking *we* need to sort through this pile," I whisper. "There's probably a lot of important information in here about where the treasure is."

"Did you listen at all to what Mom just said?"

"Of course I did."

"You don't believe her? That Grandpa's illness made him obsess over something that wasn't true?"

"No."

We look at each other for a few seconds and then Frankie says, "Me either." But I don't think she's telling me the whole truth.

We page through books and examine maps without really knowing what we're looking for. Everything is dated, but we have no idea what is what and if it even has to do with our island or some other place Grandpa explored. But then I find a journal that's only about ten years old and labeled OCRACOKE BOTANICALS. When I flip through it there's page after page of hand-drawn trees, leaves, and flowers. It doesn't seem like something Grandpa would usually do. "Look at this, Frankie."

She takes the book from me and flips through it. "Wow, he was such a good artist."

"Why was he drawing all those trees and plants?" I ask.

"I don't know. Maybe he was studying them? He wrote down their scientific names." She points out one. "These are all Latin. We learned about it in science."

"Mom knows Latin," I say, but shrug it off. We can't ask *her* anything. Not that it matters. We're not looking for a plant. We're looking for gold. I toss the book back on the table. If Grandpa wanted us to find the treasure, why would he have made this so hard?

Dad walks in and asks us how we're doing. He looks

down at the table and says, "Oh, wow, look at the treasures you found."

"Mom got them out," Frankie says. "She's trying to sort through and pick out the important stuff but decided to let you do it."

Dad kind of waves at it. "Tell you what, do you want any of it?"

Frankie and I both nod.

"Go ahead and pick three favorite things each. Let Jolene do the same. The rest is going to be boxed up tonight and donated to the museum and Mrs. Taylor can decide if it's worth keeping." Then he heads into the kitchen and it sounds like he's putting dishes away between sniffles.

Frankie and I spend the next several minutes trying to decide what we want. I realize how hard it had to have been for Mom. I end up keeping a big sketchbook of maps of North Carolina, a huge rolled-up star chart, and a puzzle book like the ones Grandpa used to give me in church, only this one he was making himself and never finished. Frankie keeps a journal about one of Grandpa's shipwreck searches, a dive log, and a diving lexicon, which is basically a dictionary about scuba diving in the ocean. She loves swimming, so that makes sense even though I think it's kind of a boring choice.

Then I grab the plant sketchbook too.

"That's four things," Frankie whispers.

"Like they will even know. Grandpa's drawings are so pretty. The museum is not getting them."

"Then I'm keeping this too," she says, and grabs one last leather journal with a picture of a lighthouse etched on the front. "I like the cover."

"That's as good a reason as any," I say.

"I hope we made good choices," Frankie says.

I look back at the huge pile of Grandpa's belongings that will now get boxed up and sent to Mrs. Taylor. We'll always be able to visit, but it's hard to see them go.

"Me too." Flipping through the plant sketches again to admire Grandpa's drawings, something occurs to me. The handwriting is different. Instead of Grandpa's normally loopy writing, these letters are blocky and very small.

"Frankie, did you ever see Grandpa write like this?" I show her the pages.

She shakes her head, but doesn't seem to be bothered. "Maybe he had different styles for different projects. I'm going to go put this stuff in my room."

I nod as Frankie walks up the stairs, turning the book over in my hands and opening the back cover, starting from the end. The last sketch is of an oleander flower. In the bottom right corner there's a date and a blocky signature.

Dunmore Throop, 1985

I stare at it for a long time, trying to figure out how Throop's book got in Grandpa's things.

Did Throop give it to him?

Did Grandpa *steal* it?

Are there more of Throop's things in the piles?

I don't have time to sort through anything more, because Mom calls down to me to tell me to wash up for dinner. I close the book, slide it between the others in my stack, and head to my room thinking that one thing I know for sure is I'm not telling anyone what I found just yet.

Just in case the answer to my second question is yes.

Just in case Grandpa stole it.

Carousing with Landlubbers

Monday is the worst day of the week. School is not my favorite place in the world, even though Dad works there. He teaches high school science. He leaves earlier than we do in the morning, so he's already gone by the time we head out the door with our skateboards. This morning before he went to work, he left a chain on the counter for Grandpa's ring so I can wear it to school.

It's such a pretty morning, warm and a little damp from the rain. Everything smells like the ocean washed up into town overnight, a musky, salty smell. Gulls everywhere grab whatever crawled out of the ground, tiny little ghost crabs, and trash people left behind. Makes me want to run to the beach and spend the day there instead. Or better yet, stay home alone and go through the rest of Grandpa's notebooks looking for more clues.

As Frankie skates us to school, I drag a stick in the sand alongside my board.

"Savannah, you're slowing us down," she scolds.

"Kinda my goal," I say.

"Well, knock it off. I'm not going to have another tardy because of you. We've only had two weeks of school. I want perfect attendance this year."

"'I want perfect attendance this year,'" I mock, and throw the stick into the scrubby brush on the side of the road. "What's so great about perfect attendance?" I ask her, but she ignores me. "Do you get a large sum of money at the end of the year? Being late is not missing a day anyway." Still ignoring me.

Jolene's sprawled out on her board humming her pirate song, with her eye patch on the top of her forehead. Mom said she had to keep it off her eye for school so she could see the board properly. Jolene had a fit. This was the compromise.

Everyone else is walking to school too. Ahead of us are Peter and his friend Colin. And Kate and LouAnn, who might walk with me now but I'm too afraid to find out. Frankie calls out to her friends Ashley and Dawn to wait up.

"Keep your arms and legs inside until your vehicle comes to a full and complete stop," I announce into my hand when Frankie hops off her board. Jolene and I roll to a stop. I pretend to put on the brake and hand Frankie the rope, and she ties our boards to the rack outside the school building. Dad's bike is already parked there.

We probably have the smallest school ever built. It's a tiny gray building with wood siding, like nearly every building on the island. Only this one has an American flag out front so you know it's something important. Sometimes I wonder what it would be like to go to one of those giant three-story brick buildings with the loud bells and huge cafeterias and hundreds of kids like I've seen in movies, but I think that might end up being way too much school for me to handle. Here we're like a family. We've all grown up together and usually all get along. Although I messed it up a bit when I pushed Kate.

Frankie waves to Ryan and then ditches us and runs in with her friends, which leaves me to walk in with Jolene. Kind of annoying, but at least I'm not walking in alone every day. That would be worse.

I walk Jolene to her room and then trudge to my own. I like my teachers enough, it's just I'd rather be looking for a clue as to why Grandpa's elbow riddle is important. There're probably more codes in the map and I really wish I could go through the rest of Grandpa's books, but all the homework is going to totally get in my way! Who wants to go home and practice fractions when you could go fishing or walk to the beach or, most important, look for buried treasure? Besides, I'm pretty sure if pirates had kids they wouldn't go to school. They'd learn everything they need to know on the ship.

"Savannah Dare?" my teacher, Mrs. Erickson, calls out. I didn't even realize all the seats had filled in around me already. Kate and LouAnn sit on the other side of the room since we sit alphabetically. Everyone looks at me as I raise my hand to show Mrs. Erickson I'm present.

"How are you doing this morning, sweetheart?" The sound of her voice makes my face turn red.

I reach for Grandpa's ring and hope she doesn't ask me any other questions. "Fine."

She moves on without saying anything about Grandpa, but I know that's what she's talking about.

Then she calls on Peter, who sits right next to me. Even though he's a year older, he's in my class because our school is so small. Fifth and sixth grades are in the same room.

"Yes, ma'am," he answers. Mrs. Erickson asks him how he's doing and he has the same answer as me. No matter what happens in this town, everyone knows. Everyone knows each other and secrets and rumors spread in the air like pollen in the spring.

After attendance and the pledge, we're off to the races. Although instead of a racehorse, I'm more like a donkey. And all day long I cannot sit still.

I sharpen my pencil thirteen times.

Get a drink twice.

Go to the restroom during every class.

I don't learn anything new. But that's okay because we learned all this stuff last year anyway.

At lunch we're allowed to go home but we usually bring lunches and sit at a picnic table outside. We don't have a cafeteria. Frankie lets me sit with her and her friends because she knows my worst fear is eating alone. It's an agreement we have—I keep her secret about the summer surfing with Ryan and she makes sure I always have a place to sit. Thing is, I'd keep her secret anyway.

I drop my ham-and-cheese sandwich on the table across from Frankie's friends Ashley and Dawn. Ashley has different color nails every single day because her mom owns the nail salon in town, and Dawn always smells like coffee because her mom owns the coffee shop. My sisters and I might be the only kids at the table whose parents don't own a business in town. Between Mom's research and lectures, Dad's teaching, and Grandpa's treasure hunting, we probably smell like books and beakers and ink and sailing ships.

Frankie and I can't talk about our plans for the afternoon, so we write notes down on a piece of paper and pass it back and forth under the table while Frankie pretends to listen to Ashley and Dawn.

Me: Maybe the answer is in the rest of Grandpa's stuff.

Frankie: Why wouldn't he have made that clear?

"And then my mom actually wanted me to wear that horrible purple polo," Ashley says. "I don't wear purple."

"Purple is horrendous," Frankie says.

Frankie: We could ask Dad.

Me: Seems risky.

"But you look so good in purple," Dawn says. "It goes great with your hair."

"You really think so?" Ashley asks, flipping her hair.

"Yeah, purple is so pretty." Frankie nods as she passes me the paper.

Me: We can't let them donate all of it to Mrs. Taylor before we know exactly what's going on.

Frankie: We may never figure this out.

"Why do you look like you're going to kill your sister, Savannah?" Dawn asks me, forcing me to take my evil eye off my sister.

"Because she knows how much I despise purple," I say, and gather up my books to head to science.

"What's her problem?" Ashley whispers as I leave. But I don't hear Frankie's answer.

The rest of the day is more of the same. Two minutes

before the last bell rings, I'm completely packed and ready to go home. Mr. Baranski says, "Savannah, the bell hasn't even rung yet." But before he can get a response from me, the bell does ring and I'm out of my seat, down the hall, and outside by our skateboards in four seconds flat.

Kate and LouAnn come out together and as they get closer, my breathing gets faster. I know I should apologize for last year, but I can't seem to get the words out. Both girls sort of give me a half-smile as they pass but nobody says anything.

It's a special kind of awful.

When Jolene and Frankie finally get there, I ask them what took so long.

"Jolene had a class trip today. They got back late and had to get everything together," Frankie says as she zips Jolene's backpack. "Calm down, okay?"

"We're running out of time." I pass Jolene her board and Frankie hers and we line up and head home. "I want to know what we're supposed to do."

"So do I, but you also have to be prepared to not know."

"I don't like not knowing," Jolene says.

"No one does." Frankie pulls us home, and the entire time I think about elbows and Dunmore Throop's signature in that book. Nothing makes sense. I'm starting to get a little mad at Grandpa for making this so confusing.

When we get home, Dad is loading something into

a strange car. I know whose it is before we even come to a stop. His green hat gives him away. And my dad is giving him a table lamp Grandpa made from a rusty lantern from a ship.

"What are you doing?" I yell when we reach the driveway. I grab the door of the car and startle my dad.

"Savannah Mae! What in the world are *you* doing?" He looks at me with such disappointment that I don't say anything. I glance at Throop, who almost looks like he's smiling at me. But not in a nice way. In a way that seems to say, "You lose, I win."

"Apologize to Mr. Throop, please," Dad says, "for so rudely grabbing his door and shouting at us like you've been raised in a barn."

"It's quite all right," Mr. Throop says. "The child was taken by emotion. There's no harm in a little passion."

My dad disagrees and tells me to apologize again.

"I will not," I say, and run into the house and up to my room, where I slam the door extra hard. Slamming the door never does anything but it feels good anyway. Usually Dad will come and check on me. But this time he doesn't. I watch out the window as Dad and Mr. Throop talk in the driveway. Dad has his arms crossed and he nods while he looks at the sand. Mr. Throop waves his hands around and even points at my dad. My dad is a teacher! You don't point at teachers.

I don't know what it is, but there's something about this Throop guy I don't like.

May Day, May Day!

An entire week goes by and we can't find any more clues in Grandpa's stuff. Every day after school, I sit in the crow's nest and go through Grandpa's journals—the ones I'm allowed to keep and the ones left in boxes that will be going to Mrs. Taylor next weekend. Everything is sprawled around me on the floor. But most of the entries are about trips he took when he was a young man and have nothing to do with Ocracoke or Blackbeard.

Frankie and Jolene help a little bit, but they both get bored and end up doing other things. One evening Dad peeks upstairs and asks me what I'm up to.

"I just like reading about what Grandpa did," I said. "He went on a lot of adventures."

"Yes, he definitely did."

"How did he do it?"

"Do what? Travel?"

"Figure out where everything is, like shipwrecks and stuff?"

"Well, you remember his boat, right? He used to have all kinds of equipment for that sort of thing. Kind of like Uncle Randy's fishing boat with the radar."

"He didn't have to crack codes or follow treasure maps."

"No." Dad smiled. "He liked that sort of thing for fun mostly. Look, Sav, I came up because your mom and I actually have to talk to you girls downstairs. Your sisters are already down there."

I look up at him over my book. "Another family meeting?"

"Yeah."

I sigh and follow him downstairs. He sits next to Mom on the couch. Mom looks worried when she sees me.

"They've had a lot this week, Jack. Maybe this should wait."

But Dad shakes his head and holds Mom's hand. "I like things out in the open. The girls are smart and strong. They will understand." He looks at the three of us lined up on the bench Grandpa salvaged from an old sailing ship. Jolene swings her feet. Frankie and I glance at each other. Whatever it is, I hope Dad's right.

"I'm just going to say it and not keep you girls in suspense any longer." He lets out a long breath. "We have to sell the house. We're going to be listing it as soon as possible, so we only have a few weeks to go through everything, sell what we can, give away what we can. And, of course, find a new place to live."

Jolene's feet stop.

"Sell the Queen Mary?" I squeak out, hardly believing what I'm hearing. "Selling Grandpa's things is bad enough, but the whole house? *Our* whole house?"

Frankie starts twirling her hair but doesn't say anything at all.

Jolene bursts into tears and runs into Mom's arms.

My insides seem to disappear. Like I've turned into a hollow ghost with no lungs to breathe. I feel like I might throw up.

"But I've lived here my whole life," Jolene says through her sobs. "Why do we have to move?"

"It's complicated, sweetheart, but mostly it's because we can't afford the house," Mom says. She has tears in her eyes too. "We were struggling as it is. I'm so sorry, girls."

"Are we going to stay in the village?" Frankie asks.

Mom and Dad look at each other. Dad says, "We wish we could, but Dunmore says this house will sell very fast, probably to someone who wants to turn it into a vacation home, which is the best deal we can hope for. And considering there's nothing small for sale that we can afford right now, we will probably have to move to the mainland."

I stare at Dad. "Who is this Dunmore Throop guy

anyway? And why does he get to decide what to do with everything in our lives?"

Mom gives me a warning look to lower my sails. "He doesn't get to decide everything in our lives, Savannah."

"Mr. Throop was Grandpa's business partner," explains Dad. "Everything that Grandpa owned is half his. At least he says it is. We're trying to find all the documents."

Frankie and I stare at each other.

"On top of that, our half of the inheritance is supposed to be split with Uncle Randy," Mom says.

"'Hairy dance,'" I mumble, and press myself deeper into the cushions. *Now* I understand what Jolene overheard. Uncle Randy talking to Throop about his half of the inheritance.

"What?" Mom asks.

"Nothing."

"Frances?" Dad says. "What are you thinking?"

"I don't know what I'm thinking," Frankie says quietly, looking at the old trunk we use as a coffee table instead of looking at Mom's or Dad's face. I think she's trying to be smart and strong like Dad said we would be.

I stand up. "Well, I know what I'm thinking!"

"Please don't shout, honey," Mom says.

But I don't listen. "I'm thinking this is the worst idea I've ever heard! Grandpa would be so mad if he knew what you were doing!" I stomp my way up the stairs, ignoring their calls for me to please come back so we can all talk. What is there to talk about? They've obviously already made up their minds. No thanks to Throop.

I hear Mom say to Dad that they should've waited a little longer and let everything settle before they told us. Dad says, "And then shake everything up all over again? No. Sav will be okay. She needs some time."

But he's wrong. I slam my door to prove it. Time will not make this better. Nothing can make this better. I throw myself down on my bed and cover my face with a pillow.

A few minutes later there's a knock at my door and Dad lets himself in.

"Sweetheart, can we talk?"

"About what?" I mumble from under the pillow.

"About what you're feeling right now. I know you're angry."

"I don't want to move, Dad."

"I know. None of us want to. But there's only so much we can do."

I move the pillow and look at him. "Can't you and Mom get better jobs? Run a fishing business like Uncle Randy?"

He smiles. "You know it's not that simple here. There aren't a lot of options for jobs."

"Then we'll all get jobs. Frankie can lie about her age and be a lifeguard, I can work with Mrs. Taylor at the museum, and Jolene can . . ."

"Frankie's not going to be a lifeguard until she's fifteen. Jolene's too little to have a job. And so are you. But I appreciate your ambition." Dad smiles, but it doesn't cheer me up at all.

"Grandpa would be so mad if he knew you were doing this."

"He'd be disappointed, yes. But he knew this was a possibility. We talked about it before he died and it's been the backup plan for several months. Your mother and I had hoped we might be able to squeak through, but we've sat down with Uncle Randy and we've all come to the conclusion that selling is the best way to go for the whole family. Mr. Throop will get his share and we will all move forward."

"But it's not fair that our cousins don't have to move, too." The words seem stuck in my throat. "And there's not enough time."

"Not enough time for what, sweetheart?" Dad asks.

But I don't tell him about the map Grandpa left us. He'd never understand why it was so important to me.

"We're all going to be okay, you'll see," he says. "It'll be a big change, but if anyone can handle it, it's you, Savvy, my little tiger shark." He smooths my hair out of my face and pulls me to his chest for a huge Dad-hug. It does make me feel better, but what would really make me feel better is if I knew what Grandpa had been thinking when he was still alive. If he knew this was a possibility and still left us the map, then he knew we could solve it quickly.

I've got to work faster.

It's the only way to keep the Queen Mary from going down.

The First Duel

By the weekend we still haven't found anything that connects to the elbow riddle despite working on it every day after school. On Sunday, Mom asks us to help haul the boxes off to Mrs. Taylor at the historical society. She's gotten everything packed that she thinks the museum might like. Everything in my body feels as tightly packed as Grandpa's boxed-up books. I'm dreading it, but she says we all need to pitch in together. Frankie and I tie our boards together and load two boxes on them and Mom pulls a big wooden wagon. Jolene skips behind all of us, holding on to Py's leash, getting out of doing the work, as usual.

On the way across town we pass families on bicycles heading to the beach, and families visiting shops near the harbor at Silver Lake, mostly visitors. Eventually, we take a turn down a little side street. A loud *honk* from a boat out in the bay echoes across the water—we can see it through the few trees. Uncle Randy and Peter wave from the deck. I'm the only one who doesn't wave back.

Mom and Frankie say hello to everyone we know, which, other than the vacationers, is everyone. I don't feel like talking, though. One of the high school teachers who works with Dad stops Mom and talks for a little while about Grandpa. Jolene holds on to Py's leash and picks flowers on the side of the road while they talk. "My condolences to your family," the woman says, and gives us all hugs.

"Thank you," Mom says, and once the lady is gone, Jolene asks, "What's 'condolences'?"

"It means she's sorry for our loss."

"I have condolences, too," Jolene says.

"I know you do, baby." Mom bends down and picks three of the red-and-yellow daisies that grow all over our sandy yard and the sides of streets. "It's nice to know people cared about Grandpa so much, isn't it?" She puts one flower behind each of our ears like she used to when we were little, when she'd pull us in the wagon before Frankie learned how to skateboard. "I've always loved this pretty little flower. I bet our new home will have them too," she says. She kisses each of us, picks up the handle of the wagon, and says nothing more until we reach the museum. She sounds like she's already left Ocracoke.

Mrs. Taylor is so excited when we come in. "This is such a privilege," she says. "You could have chosen any bigger museum to house all of these incredible historical documents."

"Grandpa Cornelius loved to work here, Evelyn. His things belong to Ocracoke," Mom says. I don't like the way she says it. It sounds so final. We're leaving his things behind and we're leaving the village. We belong to Ocracoke too. Doesn't she understand that?

Mrs. Taylor clasps her hands together. "It's a history nerd's dream come true. I will be exceptionally careful with everything."

We unload the boxes onto the floor for Mrs. Taylor, and she gingerly opens one and begins to lift things inside to see what they are. She picks up an old book, gasping nearly every time she turns a page, and even smelling a lot of them. "There's nothing like old, well-loved books," she says. Mom smiles. Even Frankie smiles. Jolene twirls around with the dog. I want to hit someone.

"Well, the girls and I have to get going, but you know who to ask if you have any questions about anything," Mom says. She holds Jolene's shoulders and guides her and Py out. Frankie says goodbye and follows.

"Mom, I'm going to stay and help Mrs. Taylor sort through the boxes," I say.

"Savvy, I'm sure she doesn't need your help right this minute," Mom says, motioning for me to follow.

"Oh, actually it would be quite nice to have Savannah

help, if you can spare her," Mrs. Taylor says. "She can help rearrange some of the books in the upstairs library to make room." She smiles at me. She has more wrinkles around her eyes than Mom, but she has a really friendly smile. Even her wrinkles smile.

"All right, then. I think that would be very nice," Mom says. "God knows the girl can hardly sit still. Maybe this will give her some focus."

"Thanks, Mom, I think," I say. Mom kisses my forehead.

"Be good," she says.

When she and my sisters leave, Mrs. Taylor and I sit on the floor and start pulling things out of the boxes. I tell her what each and every book, paper, map, and note-pad is, whether I actually know what they are or not. It all sounds smart coming out of my mouth. I am good at talking, after all. And I don't think she minds.

"You were very close to your grandpa, weren't you, Savannah?" Mrs. Taylor asks.

That kind of makes all of my words stop, so I nod.

"I can tell," she says. "You know his work so well."

"He wanted me and my sisters to keep it all," I say, trying to not sound angry because Mrs. Taylor is so nice and it's not her fault we're getting rid of everything.

"Then why in the world did you bring it all here?" she asks, placing her hand on my arm.

"Because my parents say they can't pay for the house

by themselves so we have to move and can't bring it all with us."

"Oh darlin', I had no idea." Mrs. Taylor sits back and wraps her arms around her knees. She stares at me. My eyes sting. I make myself busy going through the next box and explain that this set of maps was from the 1800s and . . .

"You know, Savannah, sometimes folks are successful in keeping their home if they can get it listed as a historical property. That's how this house became a museum. In fact, it was moved here to make sure it could be saved."

"How do you get a house listed like that?" I ask.

"Homes that are really old, or on property that's famous for some reason, can be protected by the government. Your home, after the lighthouse, is the oldest building in the village. Years ago I tried to convince your grandfather to get it registered but he didn't want anyone's hands near his work, especially not the government, which I understood, but now . . ."

"Everything inside it is even older than the house," I say. "It's like its own museum already."

Mrs. Taylor holds a finger up and presses her lips together. "Now that's something to consider. It should all be preserved. It's going to be a lot of research and I'll have to talk to your parents about it." She folds up one of the now-emptied boxes. "But enough about that. I'll take care of everything. For now, let's continue to cata-log these things so that nothing is lost."

"Okay."

We manage to clear out all the boxes and bring everything up to the third-floor library. Mrs. Taylor and I make room on several shelves for Grandpa's books and journals. She says eventually she will go through everything very carefully and document every last page, but for now everything is safe and sound in the library. And we can visit and go through it whenever we want since we're family. I like that idea.

The little bell downstairs rings when someone walks in the door. Mrs. Taylor excuses herself while I fold up the remaining boxes. I can hear her say good morning to someone as I walk down to say goodbye.

"You would not believe the collection that just came in," she says.

"Is that so?" The man's deep voice is familiar. He's not from town and I recognize it immediately.

"Yes, a local treasure hunter named Cornelius Dare. Once I get it organized, I'll have an exhibit for the public."

"Sounds most intriguing," the man says, and I can already picture his green hat. Why is he pretending he doesn't know Grandpa? Mrs. Taylor must not know he used to work with Grandpa. I come into the room to say goodbye and Mrs. Taylor hugs me as I stare at Throop. He doesn't say anything and neither do I. *Of course it's intriguing,* I think. It's Grandpa's stuff and he *better* keep his hands off it.

I say that last part out loud. By accident.

Both of them look surprised.

"Savannah," Mrs. Taylor says, nervously laughing. "I'm sure Mr. Throop would never do anything to harm historical artifacts."

"Of course not," Mr. Throop says. "Evelyn, you wouldn't have happened to get a copy of that document I requested last week, did you?"

"Oh yes, we did! One moment, it's on my desk upstairs. Let me go grab it." She runs up the steps and leaves me with Mr. Throop in the hallway. I have nothing more to say to him, so I make an annoyed sound and turn to go, but he grabs my arm.

"Hey!" I yank it away, quickly.

He puts his hands in his pockets. "Calm down, lass, I only wanted to say, before you left, that things will go much smoother from here if you let me handle it."

"Handle what?" I ask.

"Your grandfather's . . . affairs."

"What are you talking about?" I ask him, even though I have a sinking feeling he's talking about Blackbeard's treasure.

He bends down to my level and puts his garlic-smelling face way too close to mine. "Whatever is in that map he left you."

I stare at his dark, gray eyes and use my best lying

voice. "I don't have any idea what you're talking about."

Before he can say anything else, Mrs. Taylor's footsteps are in the hall.

"Oh, Dunmore," she says. "Tell Savannah . . ."

But I'm out the door before she can finish.

14

The Elbow Tree

I run the entire way home. All the way back around Silver Lake, down the sidewalk, and up my front porch, and then I burst in the door.

"Mom! Dad! Dunmore Throop is trying to steal Grandpa's treasure!"

Everyone is gathered around an enormous pile of Grandpa's clothes on the couch. All their heads jerk toward me.

"Savvy. Please," Dad says. "Lower your voice."

I run up to him and try to catch my breath. "You don't understand. He told me . . . he knows about the map . . . he told me in the museum that he was going to get to Blackbeard's treasure first. Well, he didn't say exactly that but it was close. I can tell what he meant because he's a sinister villain, a scallywag, a real bilge rat, I know it, and . . ."

"Darling," Mom says as she folds a pair of pants. "Breathe."

"What's a bilge rat?" Jolene asks.

Frankie stares at me like she can't believe what I've just done. I can't believe it either, but I'm so desperate I let it slip.

"I thought we already discussed this. There is no buried treasure," Dad says. "What map are you talking about?" He drapes a button-down shirt of Grandpa's on the chair near me and I can smell Grandpa in it—salty air and his minty aftershave. For a second it makes me forget what I was yelling about. But only for a second. I run upstairs, grab the tube with the map, and run back down.

"Sav!" Jolene whispers. "It's supposed to be secret."

"No secrets," Mom says. "I forbid it."

I unroll the map and show them. "Grandpa showed me this a while ago and then he left it in the crow's nest for us. I'm sure of it. I found it up there a few days before he . . ." I don't say it. They know what I mean. "I think he knew someone had to take care of it. Finish his quest."

Mom examines the map, gently running a finger over the crinkly paper. "It's beautiful," she says. "One of his best, don't you think, Jack?"

Dad nods. He smiles at my sisters and me. "Grandpa left you a gorgeous gift. But it's not real, Savvy."

"Yes, it is, Dad," Frankie finally chimes in. She runs upstairs and grabs the envelope from Mrs. Taylor.

"What's with all the running?" Mom sighs, but she

pulls her hair up into a bun and puts on her reading glasses. Frankie shows them the code and the poem. Mom and Dad look at each other for a long time, like they're trying to figure something out.

"See!" I yell. "Don't you see? He wanted us to find the treasure because he got too old to keep looking. He couldn't get to it and he knew we could. Now we can't move or Throop will get it first!"

"Savannah, sit down," Mom says.

"I don't want to sit."

Her eyebrow speaks. I pick up Grandpa's shirt and sit in the chair. I wrap the soft, worn fabric around my hands to keep from fidgeting.

"We know you don't want to move," Mom says. "But you're making this much harder on us than I think is fair. We don't want to go either. The Queen Mary, the village, it's been our home for so long. But sometimes you don't have a choice and that's where we're at."

I want to argue that that's nice and all, but what does that have to do with the treasure?

Then Dad comes over to me and crouches down. "This is one of Grandpa's games for you three, don't you see? One last puzzle for you to solve even after he was gone, so that in a way he could stick around a little bit longer for you." Tears form in the corners of Dad's eyes. I start shaking my head but he holds my face in his hands and stops me. "Yes, Savvy, it's a game. The man was a genius and his heart was full of love for you girls."

Frankie's crying now, very quietly, and I can hear her breathing slow as I stare at Dad, trying to change the words he's said into something I actually want to believe. It doesn't explain what Throop said to me. And in my head I chant to myself, *It's not true, It's not true, It's not true.* But Dad is very convincing. What if he's right?

"Why would Grandpa make us think it was real, then?" Frankie asks between sniffling. "He'd have said it was a game in the letter. He never lied to us."

Frankie's words give me hope. "Yes!" I say. "That's true."

Dad rubs the tears off his stubbly cheeks and stands up. With one arm around his middle and the other seeming to hold up his head, he sighs and turns to Mom. "What do you think, Anne?"

"I don't know what to think. Just let them enjoy it, Jack." She picks up another pair of Grandpa's pants. "There's no harm."

They still don't believe me. But I don't say anything else. Nothing about the map as I roll it back up and slip it into the tube, and nothing about Throop, who I still think is after it. Frankie is totally right, whether Mom and Dad want to believe it or not. Grandpa never lied.

"Girls, I'm going to get dinner started soon. Go wash your hands, please," Mom says. Frankie takes Jolene's hand and we all head upstairs without saying anything. After Frankie and I put away Grandpa's things, we all gather in the bathroom. It's small, but we squeeze in around the sink. I turn on the water so it sounds like we're washing up and no one can hear us talk.

Jolene says, "Grandpa wouldn't lie to us."

"No, he wouldn't," Frankie says. She looks at my reflection in the mirror. "Something doesn't add up."

"No, it doesn't, because Dad is wrong," I say. It doesn't feel good saying that.

"Dad's a teacher and he's *wrong*," Jolene says, like her little world has come crashing down.

"Yeah," I say. "It happens sometimes. You'll get used to it." But I wasn't sure even I was used to it yet. I still had a weird feeling, like an itch somewhere deep in my brain. I always believed Grandpa. And I also always believed Dad. But they couldn't both be right.

I lean into the sink and stare at our reflections in the mirror. I hate to admit it, but the three of us look so much alike without trying: golden-brown skin from the sun, streaky blond hair, cutoff jean shorts. Though if Frankie gets any taller, her face will be out of sight and only her long hair will hang down in the reflection. Jolene is so pretty she stands out like a little angel, even wearing the eye patch. Then there's me in the middle. Short hair. Snubby nose. Too many freckles. Average. The most piratey of us all.

I squint my eyes and squeeze my eyebrows together to look tougher. "Elbow, elbow, elbow, elbow," I say to our mirror-selves. "What does it mean, Grandpa?"

We're staring into the mirror like we're waiting for

our reflections to answer back when Jolene says, "That reminds me!" and makes me and Frankie jump. Then she runs off.

"What is she doing?" I ask Frankie.

"No idea." She hands me the soap. "Stop making that face and wash your hands for real."

"You wash your hands for real," I say.

"I already did. Yours are disgusting. Look at your nails, do you ever trim them?"

"Shut up, *Mom*," I say, but soap up my hands anyway.

Jolene comes bursting back through the door, which hits the wall with a loud *thunk*.

"I made this last week on our class trip." She's holding a piece of paper and we can tell there's a drawing on the other side.

"Well, what is it, Jolene? We don't have all night." I shut off the water and dry my hands.

"It's from when we went to the park, to learn about the 'forals and flaunas' of the Outer Banks."

"The plants and animals? I think you mean 'flora' and 'fauna,'" Frankie says.

"That's what I said."

"Uh-huh." Frankie looks in the mirror and pinches at a small pimple on her chin.

Out of big-sister duty, I ask Jolene, "What did you draw?"

She turns her paper around and shows us her mess of a charcoal sketch. But I can tell what it is—one of the enormous live oak trees in the park. It's a massive one, probably one of the oldest around.

"I remember that tree!" Frankie says, looking at the picture from the reflection in the mirror. "Grandpa took us to it once and told us stories about how the native people on the island would bend branches so that they grew into strange formations. The branches would become trail directions and would stay like that for centuries."

"Oh yeah," I say. "I remember that too." I look closer at Jolene's picture and remember the giant branch that went straight out toward the ocean, and then bent straight up and pointed to the stars. "It's a very nice tree."

"It's the Elbow Tree!" Jolene shouts. "Do you like it? Do you think I did a good job coloring it? It was a long walk and it was so hot, but when we got there . . ."

"Wait, wait, wait!" I put my hand over her mouth to make her stop talking. "What did you call it?"

"Uh ebo ee."

I take my hand off her mouth. "What?"

"The Elbow Tree."

Frankie and I look at each other. "Who told you it was called that?" she asks Jolene.

"Grandpa."

I tear out of the bathroom and my sisters follow me to my room. I grab the book Grandpa had with all the flowers and trees. Flipping through I find the sketch I knew would be there. A giant live oak in the park.

"Do you remember how to get to it?"

Jolene shrugs. "Maybe. I don't know."

"You *need* to remember *right now*!"

She almost salutes me, but stops herself. "Why?"

I turn the book around for my sisters to see the same exact tree in Grandpa's—*ahem*, Throop's—sketchbook.

"Because *that's* where Blackbeard's treasure is."

Captain Jolene
Takes the Helm

"It's the answer to the riddle," I say as we run toward the park with shovels over our shoulders. Mom tried to stop us since we'd just washed up, but I promised her we wouldn't be long. I knew that was probably a lie, but this was important and she would have to understand. Besides, they were still so distracted by sorting through things that she hadn't even turned on the oven yet. They didn't see us go into the shed for the shovels.

We jog down the street, turn left, and pass the light-house. "Don't you get it?" I say. "The Elbow Tree—the treasure has to be buried beneath the Elbow Tree. It makes perfect sense!"

"I know, I do get it, Sav, but don't you think we should wait until tomorrow?" Frankie asks. "We're not going to find buried treasure and still get home in time for bed."

"How do you know?" I ask. "Besides, so what? We

have to get started. I'll never be able to sleep if we don't at least go look."

"Stop flailing your arms around and tell me what's going on," she says. So I tell her every detail about Mr. Throop stopping me in the hall at the museum. And even about the book with Throop's signature in it.

"Are you sure he said it like that?" Frankie asks.

"I'm surer than sure," I say. "Somehow he knows about the map. He's after the treasure."

"So Grandpa stole his sketchbook of *plants*?"

"Or maybe it got mixed in with Grandpa's stuff."

Jolene runs behind us with a tiny shovel made for taking ash out of a fireplace. I ask her if she can see okay while she's running with the eye patch on and she says, "Shiver me timbers! Why does everyone ask me that?"

"Just checking," I say.

When we reach the entrance of the park, we kick off our shoes into the sand and I turn to her again. "Now it's all up to you, Captain Jolene." I salute her.

Her eyes—or eye—gets wide. Then it starts to tear up.

"Now don't cry," Frankie says. "You can do it. You can remember. Look, we'll do it bit by bit. Start walking, and when we come to a fork, you do your best to choose, okay?"

Jolene nods as Frankie wipes her tear away. And then we start to walk. The sandy trails of the park are narrow and bend this way and that, like whoever made them couldn't make up their mind which trees to walk around. We've been in nearly every inch of the park but I can't remember where that Elbow Tree is. Our footsteps are silent as we tread through, and we're surrounded by a canopy of twisted branches and moss. An occasional jay screeches overhead. Little sparrows flit off the path into scrubby bushes.

For a long time Jolene does great, shouting out left or right every time we come to a split in the trail with no hesitation. But after about the fifth turn, I can tell she's not as certain anymore.

"Do you remember how long you were walking before you got to it?" I ask her. She slowly shakes her head. "How many turns total?" She shakes her head again.

"Let's take a break and think about this," Frankie says, and we all sit on a fallen branch along the path. As usual, the mosquitoes find us as soon as we stop moving.

I dig my bare feet into the sand while Frankie strategizes. It's warm on top and cool underneath.

"I mean we've all been to the tree," Frankie says. "Jolene has the advantage of having just been there a few days ago but together we should be able to figure out where it is. The park's not *that* big."

"It was so long ago," I say, wiggling my toes in the sand. "And we always spent more time over at the beach because that's what *you* liked, instead of in the trees."

"Oh no! Don't blame me. You and Grandpa spent hours looking for coins in the surf. It wasn't all my idea!"

"That's enough!" Jolene shouts. "I remember!" And she gets up and starts walking away from us. We quickly scramble after her, sending sand everywhere. After several more minutes, and right before I'm about to lose my mind completely, Jolene stops dead in her path. We almost run into her.

"There it is."

It's a very dense part of the park and the trees all run into each other so it's hard to tell where one tree ends and the other begins; the branches are all intertwined like clasped fingers.

But when you look closely, there is one tree that stands out.

We look up at the giant live oak towering over us. Its branches twist in every direction like it couldn't remember which way the sun was, all of them knobby, gnarly elbows and knees with massive curtains of moss draping down like long hair.

"I remember now," I say, twisting Grandpa's celestial ring between my fingers.

Grandpa had called the tree "a weeping old woman" on one of our walks. "She's waiting for her sailor who is never coming home."

"Who's the sailor?" I whispered.

Grandpa made his voice low and wobbly. "Nobody knows. A pirate maybe?"

The branches creaked around us. "Are there a lot of ghosts in here?" I asked.

"In the woods?" Grandpa leaned down close to me. "Not many. Maybe Blackbeard's. He's all over the island though. I imagine he occasionally meets up with Theodosia at the lighthouse."

Theodosia is another famous ghost in town, but I've never seen her. "Why?"

"Both looking for something, I suppose. Blackbeard's lost ship, Theodosia's family."

"Theodosia," I repeated, enjoying the sound of her name on my tongue. "As long as they're nice, I'm not afraid."

"Ghosts are only stories that want to be told." Grandpa hugged me close. "No reason to be afraid. Especially near a tree as beautiful as the weeping old woman."

Or, as he must have named it for Jolene at some point, the *Elbow* Tree. She runs up to that elbow now and tries to reach it. One branch on the left of the trunk unnaturally twists and turns straight up, where the others meander their way around each other like they're lost. She can only touch it with the tips of her fingers.

"You're a genius, Jolene," I say, and she bounces up and down. "Now let's dig."

"Where?" Frankie asks. "It could be anywhere. This tree is huge."

"Has to be under the elbow itself."

Frankie nods. "Okay. Let's do it."

We start to dig a wide hole under the elbow, fighting to keep the sand from falling back inside. Our shovels clank against each other and I know there has to be a better way, but we keep going because I don't know what that way is yet. After a while, Jolene starts whining. "I'm sweaty."

"Pirates aren't afraid of a little sweat," I say. "Keep digging."

Sand flies in every direction and the sun drops lower in the sky, beneath the tree branches. I don't even realize how late it's getting until I look up and see the shadows dancing around the paths. And then, out of the corner of my eye, there's some kind of shadowy movement behind another tree. Most often the animals we see roaming around are birds or cats. But this something is bigger than a bird or cat.

"Stop!" I whisper-yell at my sisters. They freeze and look up.

"What is it?" Frankie asks.

I point in the direction where the shadow moved. Frankie looks and squints, but neither of us sees anything now.

"Your imagination," Frankie says.

"Probably," I admit.

We're about to start digging again when a twig snaps loudly behind us. Like someone stepped on it with a very big foot. Ocracoke is isolated. Except for the wild ponies, the biggest feet belong to people. And the wild ponies aren't anywhere near the village. They have their own pen and free-roaming pastures at the north end.

Jolene runs over and hides behind us.

"Probably someone else walking the trails," Frankie says, standing in front of both of us. "Hello?" she calls out.

Somewhere a dog barks.

The ocean waves in the distance seem to say, *Hushhh hushhh.*

When I try really hard, I think I can make out some kind of shape between the scraggy bushes, but it's like a cluster of stars: If you try to look directly at it, it seems to disappear.

"What if it's Blackbeard's ghost?" Jolene's voice is shaky. "What if he doesn't want us to find his treasure after all?"

I consider that for a second, but then reject it. "No way. If Edward is here, he would know we only want to be the right and true guardians of this treasure."

"Who have now decided they want to use the treasure to save their house?" Frankie whispers, looking at me and madly twirling her hair. She's going to make herself bald if she doesn't stop.

"We don't have to use all of it," I say. "Some of it can still go in a museum like we promised. I don't think Blackbeard will mind if we take a tiny cut."

"Maybe he doesn't like sharing," Jolene says. "He *is* a pirate."

A jay screeches in the tree above us. Frankie looks up. "It's a warning," she says.

I have to say, my sisters are not helping.

"Stop it! Both of you!"

I worry that they're right and I'm wrong, but as we stand there waiting, no one appears, ghostly or otherwise. Only the wind through the moss and rustling leaves of the underbrush, pushing wisps of sand across the surface of the ground. Strangely quiet.

"Let's head home for today," Frankie says. "Mom's waiting for us anyway."

"Okay," Jolene and I say at the same time.

We cover up the hole with moss and branches and hurry back through the twists and turns of the park trails, toward the road, and the streetlights, and other people, hoping to make it out of the woods before it's completely dark. We push past the tall grasses that line the park and all three of us reach the warm pavement with relief. We pull on our shoes quickly. Now, back to the Queen Mary.

Until a very tall man in a green hat steps out from behind a parked car. Throop. Again.

We hold our shovels like spears. "Why are you following us?" I ask.

Mr. Throop laughs at our weapons, his arms out like he's presenting himself onstage. "You really don't remember meeting me, do you?"

We all shake our heads.

"I met you two before this littlest Dare was even born, when I worked for your grandfather as an apprentice." He points to Jolene, who leans back against me. I put my free hand over her chest and hold her close. "You were only tiny adventurers then. Cornelius brought you aboard my ship, the *Brigantine*. You don't remember any of that?"

"No," Frankie says for all of us.

Peeking out from behind me, Jolene says, in a tiny but strong voice, "Everyone knows boats are supposed to have girl names."

Throop laughs again, but this time it sounds scratchy and annoyed. "Cornelius taught you too well, little one. But my ship is too scientific for a romantic name. I wanted it to represent something grand and majestic. It's made specifically for searching for shipwrecks. Something your grandfather and I did quite often together. At least, before he decided his ways were better than mine."

"Okay, well, that's all very nice, Mr. Throop. We have to go now," Frankie says, and starts pushing both Jolene and me forward. "We have to be home for . . ." She stops herself from saying "dinner," maybe so we don't sound so babyish. "We just have to get home."

"No worries. I'm having dinner with friends and have to be on my way as well." But he stands in the middle of the road like he's trying to block us. I'm giving him ten seconds before I hit him in the shins with my shovel. He finally starts to leave, but quickly turns and says, "One last thing. You probably don't remember this, but back in '86 a little boy was digging holes on the beach." He pauses.

"Yeah?" Frankie says. "And?"

"He was near the water and wanted to see how deep

he could make the hole. With damp sand, you know, he dug forever. He thought maybe he'd dig to the other side of the world." Throop chuckles. I hate the way it sounds, like a choking fish.

"His parents went for a walk down by the surf. Let him keep digging. They figured he was safe. Not in the water. Busy and focused."

"Not to be rude, but what's your point, sir?" I ask.

"When they returned, he'd been swallowed by the sand." Throop looks at us. I try very hard to not react. Jolene shudders under my arm.

"My point is, digging in sand is very, very dangerous without support. Cave-ins happen on beaches all the time." He pauses for a moment and, as if we don't understand what he's saying, he slowly adds, "Small children can suffocate."

The way he says it makes my skin cold.

"Who says we were digging?" I say, even though I know how ridiculous that sounds, given our shovels.

Throop shrugs. "It was only a thought. You have to be careful out there."

"Uh-huh, okay, bye now." We all mumble our goodbyes and zip around him.

But I hear the very last thing he mumbles back: "Treasure hunting is not for little girls."

Retreat to the Crow's Nest

We run home as fast as we can, past the lighthouse, past Ms. Gigantic Sunglasses putting out her trash, where Jolene pauses and says, "Doesn't she know the sun is setting?" Frankie pulls her along and we toss our shovels under the porch. We run right up the steps into the house, where Mom seems to have been waiting for us the entire time.

"All of this in and out is making me think I need to put in a swinging saloon door," she says. "Go wash up again. I've been holding off finishing dinner for you, but it's late. Uncle Randy, Aunt Della, and your cousins will be here any minute. I don't appreciate not knowing where you are."

"We were at the park, Mom," Frankie says.

"Doing what?" Mom picks up the sleeve of Jolene's shirt and drops it like it's contaminated with something horrific. She groans. "You three! Go shower and change. All of you. Thirty minutes. And, Savannah, help Jolene rinse out the shampoo!"

"Yes, ma'am," I say, and we all trudge up the stairs to follow Mom's orders. She's being extra picky, like funeral-grade, you-have-to-wear-a-dress picky. I hate when she's like this. And all for our cousins? Why should they care if we're covered in sand and dirt with leaves in our hair? That's how they always see us.

Frankie showers in our parents' bathroom and I take the hall bath. Jolene has to wait for me and then she jumps in my shower. "You want me to help you with your hair?" I ask her.

"I can do it myself," she says, and I don't argue.

"Okay, but take off that eye patch," I say as I leave the bathroom. Frankie and I wait in the attic with our hair wrapped up in towels, and we talk about Throop.

"He has some nerve!" I shout as I pace the room. Frankie sets up the Star Board but without candles this time. We're going to try to squeeze in one call to Blackbeard to see if he can tell us anything about Throop. Jolene tears into the room looking like she maybe got her hair partially wet and it's still full of soap. I'll probably hear it from Mom, but I don't care. This is more important. "Hurry up, Frankie!"

"Shhhh!" Frankie says to me. "We don't need Dad coming up here."

"But Throop has some nerve," I whisper this time. "To

try to scare us like that. To say girls can't be treasure hunters. Besides, we're not little! Who does he think he is?"

"Are you sure that's what he said?" Frankie asks.

"Of course I'm sure! Why would I make that up?"

"Shhhhh!" both Jolene and Frankie scold me.

"I don't trust him," I say as I plop down on the floor near my sisters. "He's sneaking around and watching what we're doing. I know that was him in the woods. He knows something."

"We don't know anything yet," Frankie reminds me. "Let's see what we find out. He might be looking out for us, knowing we're Grandpa's family."

"See, that's your problem, Frankie. You always think everyone is good."

"Your problem is you always think everyone is bad!"

"That's because I think like a pirate," I say.

"I don't know if that's something to be proud of," Frankie says, trying to sound like Mom.

Jolene sighs loudly. "We could ask Daddy," she says.

"No," both Frankie and I say.

I move over to the Star Board. "For now all we can do is consult Edward Teach."

There's no time for costumes or candles or polite introductions. We get right to work. We place our fingertips on the wooden paddle lightly and after we all calm down, I begin asking questions. "Please, Mr. Teach, are you there?"

For a while nothing. Just Jolene's one eye looking at

Frankie and me. "You didn't take that off to wash your face, did you?" I ask her. Jolene grins and shakes her head no.

I motion for her to close her eye.

"Show us a sign that you're here, Blackbeard."

There's a slight whistle of wind through the rafters. It's enough for me.

"Mr. Teach, I know you're listening. We mean you and your treasure no harm. You must know this by now. But we're really worried about this man, Dunmore Throop. What does he want?"

The slight whistle of wind turns to a low howl and a breeze that makes Jolene's hair flutter. She hunches down and mumbles, "I'm never doing this again. I'm never doing this again. Why do I always let you make me do this again?"

"Shhhhh," Frankie says.

My shoulders tighten and squeeze against my neck. But the window doesn't rattle like old bones this time. This time the paddle begins to move.

Jolene gasps. I shush her and repeat my question. "What does Dunmore Throop want?"

Very, very slowly the paddle moves to three different constellations.

Lynx
Orion
Ursa Minor

I know exactly which letters they translate to.

Y
O
U

Traitor Aboard
the Queen Mary

"Me?" Jolene squeaks out, and her chin begins to tremble. She hides her hands in her lap like she's afraid to touch the board again.

"No, not you," Frankie says. "If anything, he meant Savannah."

"Me?" I say. "Why me? What did I do?"

"Nothing, but you're the one who asked the question, so who else would he mean?"

"Well, maybe he meant 'you' like all three of 'you'!"

"Are you sure you didn't push the paddle, Sav?"

"I didn't do anything!"

Jolene wails. We shush her, but it's too late.

"Girls!" Mom calls up the attic steps. "Supper!"

"Sorry, Mom! Be down in a minute!" Frankie calls back. I pack up the board and slide it under the couch.

"How do you really know what those stars mean?" Frankie asks me.

"Grandpa taught me every one! There's a constellation for almost every letter of the alphabet and the ones that are missing you just have to know. Like 'Lynx' stands for 'Y.'"

She gives me a suspicious look.

"I'm telling the truth."

"Okay!" she says, but I'm not sure she totally believes me. Doesn't matter. I know what the Star Board said. Throop is after us.

The three of us sit on the couch with Jolene in the middle. Frankie gently scratches Jolene's back to get her to calm down, while I think of a plan to dig faster than ever. Before Throop can figure out what's going on.

"We should skip school," I say.

"We'd never get away with it," Frankie says. Jolene now rests her head in Frankie's lap while she combs out her wet hair. Frankie's good at getting Jolene to stop crying. "And we need to take a break from the *you-know-what*, or do it after she goes to bed."

"Nuh-huh," Jolene mumbles, not opening her eye. "I can do it."

"Then you have to stop getting so scared," I say. "Nothing bad's gonna happen to you. It's communication, like writing a letter."

"It doesn't matter," Frankie says. "We don't need the Star Board. We know where the treasure is now, so all we have to do is dig fast and hope we don't run into Throop again."

"Girls!" Mom shouts up once more and we all jump. "I'm not telling you again. Please come down to eat, our guests are all here."

Frankie and I look at each other and roll our eyes. Our cousins aren't guests. "Guests" means we have to be quiet and polite while they all talk about boring things like this year's hurricane season and the kind of kale Mom put in the salad. When we get downstairs to the kitchen, we're right: "guests" means family—Uncle Randy, Aunt Della, Peter, and Will.

But also an impostor.

Dunmore Throop.

"What's *he* doing here?" I ask. Frankie pokes my shoulder. Peter snorts.

"Savannah Mae!" Mom says. "Where are your manners? And I thought I asked you to help rinse your sister's hair?" She picks up a strand of soapy hair from Jolene's head.

"Oh, Anne, it's quite all right," Throop says. I don't like my mother's name coming out of his mouth like they're old friends. "The little lass was expecting family."

"You might as well be family," Aunt Della says, patting his hand. "Putting up with Cornelius for as long as you did." She pulls Will's baby seat buckle tighter and hands him a plastic spoon, which everyone seems to know is a bad idea except Aunt Della.

I apologize, even though I don't mean a word of it. "Nice to see you again, sir." *About as nice as getting stung by a bee,* I think to myself.

Before she sits, Frankie whispers in my ear that he must have been on his way here when we ran into him on the road. "We gave ourselves away when we ran into him, that's why he knew so much."

"It's rude to whisper, Frances," Mom says. "Save it or share it."

I want to tell Frankie to save it already. It's like she's *trying* to find a reason to believe Throop.

"Yes, ma'am," Frankie apologizes, but looks horrified that Mom used her full first name. I sit in the chair right across from Throop. I'm not taking my eyes off that man, even as I pile three chicken legs and several forkfuls of green beans on my plate. Grandpa's portrait is in the corner of my eye and he seems to be frowning.

"I would have worked with him longer, if he'd wanted me to," Throop says.

"We know," Uncle Randy says. "Dad could be . . . difficult."

"Yes, well, it was still a privilege while it lasted." Throop puts a forkful of salad in his mouth and chews too loudly. "We worked on many wonderful expeditions together through the years. I learned a lot from him."

"Did you hunt for pirate treasure together?" Jolene asks. Frankie gives me a sideways glance I pretend to not see. I keep eating my chicken leg like I'm not interested in Throop's answer, even though I'm listening very closely.

"I suppose that depends on what you consider pirate's treasure," Throop says to Jolene, smiling.

She rolls her eyes which only looks like one eye rolling because of the patch, and I almost laugh out loud, even though Mom gives her the eyebrow. "Everyone knows what treasure is," Jolene says. "Like Blackbeard's chests of diamonds and rubies and a princess tiara!"

My little sister is smarter than that. She knows that's not what real treasure hunters usually find. Some are lucky and find gold or silver coins, but usually it's artifacts like dishes and jewelry and tools. I think she's trying to throw Throop off our trail by making him think we don't really know what we're even looking for.

Throop smiles again, though this time it's smug. "Now wouldn't that be fun." He gnaws a huge piece of meat off his chicken bone and his eyes dart toward me. Nobody else seems to notice and he quickly changes the subject to the plans for the house. The grown-ups talk about a bunch of things I don't know about like inspections and escrow and mortgages.

I stop listening and focus on eating. Throop doesn't do anything else remotely mean or suspicious other than chew with his mouth open too much, so when we're all done and Mom sends Frankie and me into the kitchen to help clean up, I've got nothing good to even complain about.

"Maybe he *was* trying to look out for us in the woods," Frankie whispers as she puts the milk away. "Maybe he's just not used to kids."

"Maybe," I say. But I can't get the way he said "treasure hunting is not for little girls" out of my head. "We need to find out why he says half the house is his. I want proof."

But before Frankie can object again, I stop her. "I'm going to go ask him." I put down the plate I'm drying.

"I think you should ask Mom or Dad later tonight instead. Not make a spectacle." Frankie tries to grab my sleeve, but I ignore her. I like spectacles. Sometimes it's the only way to get straight to the truth.

When I get closer to the living room, though, I hear them talking about the Queen Mary.

"We've wanted to be sure everything ends up in the right hands," Dad says.

"Who would be better, Jack?" Uncle Randy asks. "This man knows Dad's work, they studied together. He wants nothing but the best for it. That's why we called him."

My chest squeezes at the thought of Uncle Randy and Aunt Della making plans for *my* family and *my* house and all the things that were supposed to be for my sisters and me someday. I press myself against the wall and stay very still.

"We know, Randy," Mom says. "We also have to look out for the girls. Make sure this is the right decision at the right time for everyone. Besides, Jack and I have discussed other options. For one, taking out a second mortgage to help with bills and try to keep it a little longer. In the hopes that my book will sell in the meantime and then we could give you your half of the inheritance money that way."

Yes, Mom!

"Anne, that could take a very long time—" Aunt Della starts to say, but Throop cuts her off.

"I'm prepared to offer you all cash," he says. "For the house, and everything inside it. Honestly, you'll never get another offer like this. The house is in major need of repair. And no one will want all this junk except a nostalgic old fool like me." His voice sounds like it did in the woods. Scratchy. Annoyed. I don't like it. But nobody seems to notice. I plead silently that Mom and Dad say no.

"We'll think about it," Dad finally says. "Give us a few days."

"Of course," Mr. Throop says. "Take as long as you need. I only want what's best for you and your little family."

I slide down the wall and sit on the floor.

I don't care what Frankie says. I'm skipping school.

Yo-ho! Yo-ho!
The Pirate Life Is Rough

I manage to miss two whole days before Frankie starts lecturing me.

First, she warns me I'm going to be in huge trouble when Mom and Dad find out.

Second, she says she can only cover for me for so long. She's been telling our parents that I've been staying after school for extra help in math, and telling my teachers I'm sick.

Third, she thinks I actually care about screwing up my attendance. Seriously the least of my worries. But still Frankie gets me my homework, which I've been doing late into the night so she can take it back the next day.

On Tuesday there's a call from the school office on our answering machine, but I see it before Mom does, so I erase it. Wednesday morning Frankie calls the office pretending to be Mom. She's a dead ringer.

She hangs up the phone when she's done telling them I'm home sick. "You owe me big-time. For life." She lets out a breath and stomps off.

"I'm already keeping your surfing lessons a secret," I shout after her. "So we're even."

For Thursday I'm going to have to cough up a fake doctor's note if I want to keep this up.

But I don't care. I have to do something. I have to dig.

And dig.

And dig.

But there's nothing. Only more sand. My arms hurt and I have blisters on my palms, and there's absolutely nothing to show for all my work. By Wednesday afternoon I can hardly move. After school my sisters finally come to see what I've done and Frankie says, "You have to dig *deeper*. What do you expect?"

"If I'd had some help, maybe I could have!"

"I've been busy too, you know."

"Doing what?"

"Covering for you, mostly. And I talked to Mrs. Taylor to find out if she knew anything juicy about Throop."

"Did she?" I ask.

"Only what we already know about him. She didn't know he worked with Grandpa, but I told her about it. She said all she knew was that he does a lot of research on shipwrecks and properties on the island."

"For what?"

"I don't know! Maybe he writes books like Mom."

"You'd make an awful investigative reporter."

"Good thing I have no intention of being one."

"You'd have been a better help here, with me," I say.

"I'm here now," she says, like she's a superhero. "So let's stop wasting time."

The three of us dig the rest of the day and still find nothing. The biggest problem is that we can only dig so far before the sand caves in on the hole. Just like Throop said. I hate that he was right.

"We need more hands," I say, resting my head on my arm against the tree.

"We need supports." Frankie braids her hair to get it out of her face. "Some kind of a wall to hold the sand back. The way Grandpa used to do his excavations. We could copy from one of his diagrams."

"We don't have time to build something like that," I say.

"We need one of those big yellow diggers people use when they build houses," Jolene says. She flops on the ground and takes a long drink from one of the water bottles Frankie brought.

"A backhoe?" Frankie says. "Yeah, that'd be awesome. But not likely."

But it gives me a great idea.

"Will has a toy backhoe," I say. "Remember, Uncle Randy bought him that thing when he turned three? He sits on it and tries to dig in the sand in their yard."

"We can't go steal the kid's toy," Frankie says. "Besides, it probably weighs more than all three of us."

"We'll get it in the middle of the night and pull it on our boards," I say.

"Are you serious?"

"What?"

Frankie sighs and rewraps the band at the end of her braid. I wish I could do that but my hair is still too short on account of me cutting it a few months ago when it got on my nerves. She tosses the braid over her shoulder and looks at me like she doesn't know who I am. "Skipping school, the lying, and now this?"

"We're pirates, Frankie. We have to think like pirates and act like pirates. How else do you expect us to accomplish this?"

"I don't know. I was thinking maybe legally?"

"We don't have time for laws."

"Even the pirates had laws," Frankie says. "Grandpa had it all written down in that journal I took from the pile. They had an entire code, like a real democracy."

"Okay, if this is a democracy, let's vote, then," I say. "Raise your hand if you think we should *borrow* our cousin's little backhoe—*that he will never even know is missing*—to make this work faster and easier?" Jolene's hand shoots up like a rocket and mine follows. Frankie puts her hands on her hips and gives me the big-sister look of death.

"We win," I say, and can't help but grin.

"Fine," Frankie says as we head back home to figure out a plan. "But you're taking the blame for this if we get caught. I always get in trouble for what you two do."

"Well, first of all, it can only be the two of us. Jolene is going to have to stay home," I say.

"What?" Jolene shrieks. "Not fair! I voted for you!"

"Frankie and I are going to have to sneak out in the middle of the night and dig all night. You have to stay home and be the lookout, Jolene, and cover for us if Mom and Dad suspect anything. They can't know we're gone."

"This is going to be good," Frankie mumbles.

"This is going to be ridiculous." Jolene pouts. She kicks clouds of sand with her bare feet as we walk to the fence to grab our skateboards.

"Well, I mean, if you don't think you're a good enough pirate to do it, I guess we won't be able to keep looking for the treasure," I say.

"I *am* a good enough pirate!" Jolene says.

"This is your chance to prove it," I say. "Make Grandpa proud."

"Enough, Sav," Frankie says as she pushes off. "She's got it."

"What if we don't find it, Frankie?" Jolene asks Frankie, who seems to have not heard her. Instead she's looking up ahead on the road where Ryan is waiting for her with his surfboard.

So much for helping.

Dissension in the Ranks

"Frankie," I speak extra loudly to get her attention. "One of your hearties asked you a question."

Frankie stops her board in an instant and we nearly crash into her. She whispers, "Can you stop talking like that around other people, Savannah."

"He can't hear me all the way over here," I say.

"Just stop," she says. "And don't worry, Jolene. We will find it." But she doesn't sound enthusiastic at all. She sounds faraway, like she gave up a long time ago. Just like Mom.

"You don't know that," Jolene says. "We might not."

"Jolene Dare." I bend down to her and put my hands on her shoulders. I look right in her eyes. "What would Grandpa say about that?"

"That if you think you can or can't, you're right," Jolene says.

"Exactly."

"I don't get it!" Jolene throws her hands up.

"It means if you think you can't find the treasure, you won't. But if you think you *can* find the treasure, you will," I say. "You are captain of yourself."

Jolene thinks about this and nods her head. "I'm Captain Jolene." She turns and leads us down the street toward Ryan. When we reach him, he gives Jolene a high five and smiles at all of us. "You three look like trouble," he says. He has no idea.

"I'll meet you at the beach," Frankie says, all important sounding. "I have to get my little sisters home first."

"You do not," I say. "We can *get* ourselves home."

Frankie looks at me like she might make me walk the plank.

"I'll be out in ten minutes," she says. Ryan heads in the direction of the beach and we reach our porch without another word.

When Jolene's through the front door, I turn to Frankie and say, "We *better* find it now. You can't quit."

Frankie dumps her skateboard in the sand and heads around the back of the house. I follow her. She looks worried as she talks but she's also on a mission to find something in the shed. "I've been thinking, Sav." The way she says it makes me realize she's about to say something I don't want to hear. I know this voice. "I've been thinking about what Mom and Dad said about Grandpa's games, what Throop said, what everyone says."

"What about it?"

"What if the map really was just for fun?"

"Even if that was true, that doesn't explain his letter to us," I say.

"It's possible he was blending real history with fantasy and we're chasing after nothing." She yanks our dad's old surfboard out of a corner and shuts the shed door. "He believed in ghosts."

"We believe in ghosts!"

"No, you do." She points at me, like she's blaming me for something. "You're the one who orchestrates it all. You do all the talking, you're the one who knows all the codes, you push the Star Board paddle."

"I do not!"

"It's all make-believe."

I follow her back around to the front of the house, shaking my head through her entire theory. "No, no, no, no. It is not made-up! Grandpa didn't do or say anything to make you think that when he was still here. You're letting the grown-ups trick you."

"Sav, they're not trying to trick us." Frankie sighs and hangs her head back a little bit like whatever she's thinking is too heavy for her shoulders. "It's just, I don't want to keep doing this. We don't have a lot of time left. I don't want to spend it digging holes in the woods and dressing up and talking like pirates, okay? I want to spend it with my friends."

"You mean that boy?"

Frankie's cheeks turn pink. "I mean *all* my friends." She stands on one side of the fence and I'm on the other. She shuts the gate between us.

"You're not allowed to go surfing by yourself."

"It's your turn to cover."

"What am I supposed to say?"

"I don't know. Make something up. You're good at that." She says it like it's supposed to be a compliment but it feels like an insult. "Thanks, Sav. You're the best." Then she runs down the road to meet Ryan.

Frankie seems like she's giving up and I don't know how to convince Frankie not to quit. A pirate would force her to obey, but I'm not that kind of pirate.

I sit on the porch swing and take Grandpa's ring off its chain. I open it up into its sphere shape and hold back tears as best I can but I'm so tired, it's hard. How can she give up?

A sparrow lands on the porch railing and startles me with its song. It's a Savannah Sparrow. Grandpa taught me their name on one of our walks on the trails through the scrubby wax myrtle bushes that grow all over the island. "There are a lot of sparrows in this world, but she's a sand sparrow," he said. "Hard to spot because they dart in and out of bushes all day."

"She's very cute," I said.

"You know, I've always wondered what it would feel

like to have a bird named after me," Grandpa pondered. "There's definitely not a Cornelius bird. I've searched far and wide, all over the globe for one."

I giggled. "No, you didn't, Grandpa."

"What does it feel like, to have a bird named after you?"

"It doesn't feel like anything, I guess."

"Well, it should! You and that sparrow share something special."

"We do?" I looked up at his blue eyes, still bright and friendly and full of stories. The way I always wanted to remember them.

"Sure you do. Most people overlook sparrows. There's so many of them, they all kind of look alike. There are so many other bigger, more colorful birds in the world. But the sparrow is one of the hardest workers around. Especially the Savannah Sparrow, to be able to live at the beach in harsh conditions. The heat, the storms. They have to be bold and strong."

"I didn't think of that."

"Plus, all sparrows are a sign of protection. When you see one on your adventures, you will know someone is watching over you."

"Like who? Blackbeard?"

Grandpa laughed until his face nearly turned purple. Finally he nodded and said, "Yes, actually I do believe Blackbeard watches over everyone who lives on this island."

But now, sitting on the porch of the Queen Mary, while I'll never admit it to Frankie, I'm not entirely sure I believe Grandpa about that anymore. If Blackbeard was watching over us, if *anyone* was watching over us, why was all of this happening to our family?

"What do *you* want?" I ask the little brown bird.

It hops down the railing away from me, spins and ducks and doesn't take its eyes off me.

"Shoo!"

It chirps at me one more time and flies off to a nearby branch.

We stare at each other for a long while and I think about Grandpa's words about protection. He never let me down before, why would I think he would now?

"I won't quit, Grandpa," I whisper to the bird.

I don't understand why Frankie would give up. Frankie never gives up. She knows Grandpa wasn't confused. All of the cool things he found and did throughout his life should be proof enough that he was onto something real and not a pirate fairytale. Although Blackbeard's legend has a lot of made-up stories, he was still a real pirate, with real ships. And Grandpa believed he had real treasure. I know there's something Grandpa wants us to find. Something he hid from Throop. Something we have to get to first.

"I won't let you down."

New First Mate

"Good to have you back, Savannah," Mrs. Erickson says on Thursday morning. "I hope you're feeling better."

"Much." I grin, and take my seat.

Peter taps my shoulder and whispers, "Faker."

"Shut up," I whisper back.

"I have to talk to you and Frankie at lunch."

I turn in my seat to look at his face. "About what?"

"It's about Grandpa. I'll tell you later. At *lunch*."

Groaning, I turn back around. Whatever he has to say better be worth it and not more lies about Grandpa because now I'm not going to be able to sit still all day wondering. Truth is, I'm so tired from the last three days of digging that sitting still isn't so hard. In history I almost fall asleep during a movie on ancient Egypt. Kate pokes me in the ribs to wake me up.

"Thanks."

"Hey, do you want to have lunch with us today?" she whispers.

I freeze inside. I do. So much. But Peter has to talk to me. Why does this have to happen at the same time! "I already promised Peter."

"Maybe another day." She gives me a half smile and goes back to watching the boring movie, and I'm really afraid I've missed my chance to call a parley.

At lunch, I scan the yard for Peter and find him under a tree away from other kids. He has Grandpa's walking stick propped up against the trunk. At least he's taking good care of it. I start across with my bagged lunch and when I pass Frankie, I can tell she's wondering where I'm going. But I ignore her. She wanted out, so she doesn't get to hear what Peter has to say.

"This better be good," I say as I drop into the sand next to him.

"I'm having a great day, how about you?" Peter says sarcastically.

"The last time you had something to say, it wasn't very nice." I pick the crust off my peanut-butter-and-honey sandwich and throw it for the squirrels.

"I was only telling you what my parents said. I wasn't trying to be mean."

"I know. But you shouldn't believe everything you hear."

"I don't now." Peter lowers his voice. "I overheard a conversation a couple days ago. I think you should bring Frankie over."

I look up at him and pretend I don't know anyone named Frankie. "About?"

Peter looks across the yard at my sister and back at me. "Okay. I guess you can tell her later. It's about Grandpa and Dunmore Throop. My dad was on the phone with someone, I think someone trying to sell him a fishing boat. He needs a new one and they are too expensive, so he's been calling around. Anyway, he was talking about how he's expecting an inheritance from his dad—Grandpa—and that should cover the cost . . ."

"That's it? That's not a secret."

"Give me a second to finish!" Peter takes a huge bite of his sandwich on purpose, smiling at me. I lean back on my hands and wait. And wait.

"Peter."

Still chewing and grinning at me, Peter says, "My dad said the inheritance is *in* your house."

"*In* my house?" I ask. "Like hidden somewhere? That doesn't make sense. I thought the house itself *was* the inheritance." But then I remember Throop's sketchbook. Grandpa clearly had things in the house we knew nothing about.

Peter shrugs. "He also said Dunmore Throop wants a QAR."

"I don't know what that means. Is that code for the thing that's in the house?"

Peter shrugs again. I'm getting annoyed. "I don't know what it means either," he says. "But look." He stands up, grabs the walking stick, and lays it down in the sand between us. Rolling it, he then points to some symbols at the base. Carved around the very bottom and winding up the length of the stick are the letters "QAR" repeated over and over. At each end there's a symbol for a key. The letters are linked together in a way that makes it look only like a pretty design at first glance.

"I must have examined this thing for hours after the funeral looking at all the patterns," Peter says. "I was trying to read the languages and wondering if I could learn to carve like this. I thought this was just a cool design until I heard my dad say that. For some reason it just clicked that it was actually the letters 'QAR.'"

"I'm more confused than ever." And worried about Uncle Randy keeping secrets from my parents about our own house or something hidden inside it. Why would he want us to move?

"I'm really sorry about what I said, because obviously something is going on that Grandpa only trusted you with." Peter looks down and makes designs in the sand with his fingers. "And I guess that's because he knew he couldn't trust my parents."

"We don't know that for sure," I say, even though I'm

afraid Peter could be right. "Throop might be fooling your parents. He's kind of shady, don't you think?"

"Super shady."

"Who's super shady?" a little voice says. Jolene. She holds her eye patch up so she can see us better.

"No one," I say. "Go play." She walks away with drooping shoulders.

Now I'm the one keeping all the secrets.

Grandpa had one of Throop's books.

Uncle Randy wants something in my house.

Throop wants a QAR. Whatever the heck that is.

Pretty soon I'm going to need a notebook to keep track.

"Thanks for telling me, Peter."

"No problem," he says.

I guess his truth-telling can come in handy. I probably shouldn't have been so mean to him in the past, but this is the first time the truth has helped me instead of gotten me in trouble.

Well, at least it hasn't gotten me in trouble yet.

Heave Ho!

On Friday night we tell our parents that we're having a sleepover in the attic. Frankie says even though she needs a break from the digging, she'll still cover for me. We have sleepovers all the time, so Mom and Dad don't suspect a thing anyway.

"There's not much to cover," I say as we lay out sleeping bags on the attic floor. "They'll never even know I'm gone."

"Then I'll go to bed," Frankie says, and starts to leave.

"No!" Jolene whimpers. "We're supposed to watch a movie and have popcorn."

Frankie and I look at each other and say nothing. Parley.

Mom and Dad go to bed around ten and we watch a movie about a bunch of kids who find tunnels under their town and go looking for treasure. They've got it

147

all wrong, though, 'cause pirates would not dig tunnels under a town. At least they wouldn't here in Ocracoke, or really anywhere on the coastal islands. It's all sand. No one even has basements. And I seriously doubt pirates went very far inland because they had to make fast escapes. The whole reason Blackbeard was on Ocracoke was because it was a good place to hide and then quickly sail out to the open sea. Though Grandpa said Blackbeard did visit Philadelphia once, because there's a big river he could sail up into the city. Grandpa went there himself for research, and came back with tiny Liberty Bells for all of us.

"How big was the city?" I asked him. The biggest town I'd been to was Kill Devil Hills, which is up the beach about three hours away.

"Like nothing you've ever seen, Savvy. People and cars and buses everywhere. Very noisy, but there's so much to see. So much architecture and history."

"Pirate history?"

"Some. But mostly government, music, art. One day I'll take you," he told me.

But I still haven't seen Philadelphia.

We eat way too much popcorn to try to stay awake. Jolene falls asleep, and I have to admit it's hard for me to keep my eyes open after so many days of nonstop digging and late-night homework, but I drink a *lot* of iced tea. I've got this.

Frankie shakes me awake at midnight.

"If you want to do this, you better get up," she whispers.

I yawn and pull on my backpack, partly wishing I was the one being the lookout.

"This is your last chance," I tell Frankie.

She looks hard at my face. "I don't want to do it anymore."

"Fine." My bag is heavy—full of ropes I took from the shed, in case I need to tie Will's backhoe to the board, or to use like a pulley to lift the treasure chest out of the ground. Frankie hands me a giant flashlight and I'm about to leave until I think of a better argument. "I'm never going to be able to get that thing on my board by myself. Can't you just help that much? Then I can roll it to the park and you can come back home and be cool all by yourself."

She twists her mouth into a frustrated frown and sighs through her nose. "You're exhausting, Savannah."

"You always say that."

"Because it's true. You never stop."

"You swore you'd help find and protect the treasure," I say. "Or did you forget what you promised Grandpa?"

"Shhh! Don't wake up Jolene and don't try to make me feel guilty. This was all your idea. I didn't promise Grandpa anything."

"Yes, you did!"

"No, I was mostly promising . . . you. Because you were so sad and I wanted you to feel better."

I pick at the seam on the arm of the couch. If Grandpa were here, he'd go with me. He'd lead the way. My insides hollow out just thinking about how much is gone. Even more if I'm not successful. But how am I supposed to do this without him or Frankie? A hiccup escapes.

"Savvy," Frankie says, putting her hand on mine. "Don't cry."

Of course her just saying that makes the sad and frustrated feelings bubble up and take over the whole room, squishing me on all sides. "I can't help it. Everything is falling apart."

"Not everything. We're all still together. We're going to be okay."

I grip Grandpa's ring tightly. "We are not *all* together."

"Grandpa will always be with us." Frankie pulls me close to her. I can't remember the last time she hugged me. Maybe preschool. Although that's been more my choice than hers. "Look. I'll go with you tonight, but this is it for me, okay? If we don't find anything, and I'm pretty sure we won't, I'm done. I can't do it anymore."

I wipe my nose and nod. "We will find something. I know it."

Frankie laughs. "You really are so much like Grandpa. You carry a piece of him with you just by being you."

"Really?"

"Really." She squeezes me again, straps on Grandpa's leather satchel, and says, "Come on, one last try."

We sneak down two flights of creaky steps and make sure Py doesn't bark on our way out. She just quietly wags her tail, hoping we will take her with us, but this time we can't. I tell her to go up to the attic and snuggle with Jolene and she trots right up to find her.

I've never walked around town after dark before, at least not without our parents, and never this late. As we walk, I bring Frankie up-to-date on everything Peter told me about his dad mentioning that something was in our house and about the QAR.

"In our house?" Frankie says. "He must mean the map, don't you think? There's nothing in the house that's worth *that* much."

"Maybe there is and we just don't know it."

"And what is 'QAR'? That sounds familiar. Maybe that's what's in the house?"

I shrug. Neither of us have answers.

The harbor around Silver Lake seems eerie, with the moon shining off the water, clanging boats, and clanking buoys. I imagine it's what pirates would hear and see all night long. Small waves come in from way out in the bay and lap up against the barnacle-covered docks, the shadows of gulls perched on the posts with one foot inside their rustled feathers to keep warm. It even smells different at night, a cooler, fresh smell.

All the stores are closed and dark. There's a couple sitting at the end of one dock with their feet swinging into darkness, and some vacationers here and there, but other than that there's no one around who knows us. We walk as fast as we can across town toward Peter's house.

"What if he's watching?" I ask Frankie.

"Who?"

"Throop," I say, glancing down the dark, empty streets and way out in the bay where there are a few boat lights slowly moving across the horizon, crisscrossing like planes in the night sky.

"How would he even know we're out here? Let's focus on what we need to do," she says as we reach our cousins' house. "And not get caught by Uncle Randy."

We walk around the back of their house, which sits right on the canal so they can take their boats straight to the bay. Uncle Randy's deep-sea fishing trips run all year round and we've gone out with him many times. He and Dad catch sailfish and yellowfin and fight about if the president is doing a good job or not, while we look overboard trying to find dolphins. I've tried a couple of times, but fishing is so boring and I hate seeing them flop around on the boat when they get caught. Mostly I like crashing over the waves and looking out and seeing nothing but water, like we're a million miles from home and headed straight for an open-seas adventure. I love the moment the land disappears and all you can see is blue. Blue above me, blue below.

Frankie yanks my shirt and tilts her head to tell me to move it. We creep along the side of the house. I run into a garbage can, knocking the metal lid to the ground.

It sets off a dog barking somewhere down the street and Frankie and I crouch low to the ground waiting for lights or voices or anything that says we're busted, but nothing happens. We make our way to the back.

Between Peter's house and the canal there's a swing set and next to that is the kid-sized metal backhoe Uncle Randy bought Will this summer. We roll Frankie's board up to it and she puts a foot on it to steady it. Then we try to move the thing.

We try and try and try.

"It's so heavy!" I groan.

"That's because it's screwed to the platform," Peter says behind us.

Frankie and I freeze.

"Yeah. I've been watching you for a while." Peter stands in a shadow but there's enough light that I can see his crossed arms and the smirk on his face.

The platform is covered with sand. We didn't even see the screws.

"Why are you stealing my brother's toy?" he asks.

"We're not stealing it," I say. "Only borrowing it for the night."

"Still digging in the park?"

Frankie looks at me, unsure. But I nod. Maybe Peter will help, maybe he won't. But I don't think he'll tattle after what he told me.

Peter seems to think about this for a minute. "Okay. I'm coming with you, then."

"What?" Frankie looks shocked.

"I know what you're doing and I've decided I want in."

"You didn't even believe Grandpa," Frankie says. "Why do you want in?"

"Because maybe there's some little chance that he was right. You're certainly convinced."

"She's not, actually," I say. "I just can't move this thing by myself."

"You don't believe it anymore?" Peter asks Frankie.

"I don't know what I believe."

"I don't either but I can help," Peter says. He's strong from working with his dad on the boat all the time so I know he's right, but I'm still not totally certain it's the best plan.

"You can come. But you have to work hard. You can't watch and expect to get anything out of it."

"O-kay." He looks at me like I'm talking too much. He's right. Old habits.

"Shake on it," I say. Despite how much I appreciate him telling me the truth, what if he was right and Grandpa didn't want him to know? I hope I can truly trust him. If I had my knife, I'd at least make him poke his finger and suffer a bit. Though surely Frankie would stop me.

We shake on it and then he tells us to hang on while he goes to his dad's shed.

"Do you think Grandpa would be upset about this?" I ask Frankie. "No one else is supposed to know."

"Peter is a Dare. He's family. Technically he can be part of the legend too, don't you think?"

"I guess." Frankie's right, but Grandpa didn't leave him the map. But Grandpa also never said our cousins couldn't be part of anything we did; the boys just never wanted to be. Or more often their parents wouldn't let them.

Peter brings back an enormous pair of pliers. After he works off each bolt, the three of us lug the thing onto Frankie's board and tie it down with a rope. And then we're off, rolling a miniature backhoe down the street on a skateboard in the moonlight.

I like to think Grandpa is watching from somewhere up in the stars and smiling.

Sand Ho!

As soon as we reach the Elbow Tree we get to work. Peter's eyes are wide when he sees what we've done.

"Wow. You have been really busy," he says.

"Yep."

He looks around and then at us and sighs a bit. "Not going to be easy." He sets up right where we ask—under the giant elbow—and begins digging. Frankie and I continue with shovels, pulling the sand out of the way of the digger as quickly as we can. Together the three of us make real progress.

"Cord of three," I say.

"What?" Peter pauses his digging.

"Something Grandpa used to say." I look at Frankie, who suddenly looks guilty. "That three was an important number for strength. He meant it for us sisters, but

I think it might be true for anyone. Three is a good number."

If Frankie wants out, she can be out. Peter, Jolene, and I can keep working if nothing comes from tonight. Frankie doesn't say anything and keeps digging.

An owl hoots.

A couple of hours go by. The moon and stars have disappeared behind the clouds. Even though it's the middle of the night, the air starts to feel warm and sticky like it might rain soon. Frankie braids her hair to keep it out of her face and I have to keep pushing mine back off my forehead. Sand is all over my skin, like it's becoming part of me. On top of that, I can't stop yawning.

"We don't have to do this all tonight," Frankie says.

"Yes, we do," I say. "If I only have you for one last shot, we're doing it tonight."

We have to keep repositioning the heavy backhoe so that we can get deeper into the hole, which is a pain, but it definitely digs out more sand in one scoop than we can with a shovel. Still, it's a lot of digging. Occasional flashes of lightning brighten up the trees around us. There's no thunder, but the flashes make Peter and Frankie look like skeletons. After what feels like thousands of scoops, Peter rests his head on the handles.

"Why are you stopping?" I ask.

"How long do you plan on doing this?" Peter asks.

"As long as it takes," I say.

"It could be days," he says.

"It could be," I say.

Peter sighs. "Okay, look, you can keep this thing out here for a while. Will never plays on it anyway, and if my dad even notices I'll pretend I don't know anything. But I'm going back to bed."

"Thanks, Peter," Frankie says. "We won't let anything happen to it."

"Better not. That thing cost my dad like five hundred dollars." He sort of waves and then disappears down the path. I watch his flashlight bob a little bit between trees and then the woods are dark again.

"Five hundred dollars is nothing compared to what we're about to find," I say. "We could buy five hundred of these diggers!"

"That was nice of him to help, though," Frankie says.

"It was." I sit down on the backhoe seat and dig the way Peter had been doing. "But he didn't stick around very long. I thought after what he told me he'd be more into it."

"He did a lot of work, Savannah. Got us way further than we were. For once maybe he gets it. Or even if he doesn't, he was nice to help."

"But he didn't stick around to actually find anything, so does that mean I still have to give him part of the treasure?"

"You? Don't you mean 'we'?"

Grunting, I pull the handles back to pick up sand.

"Yes, I mean 'we.' At least for tonight. If you quit, then I mean 'me.'" Controlling the backhoe is a lot harder than I realized. And since I've been digging all week, my arms are about done. My muscles burn like the way your mouth feels after you eat a hot pepper. I try again, but I'm useless. My arms shake. I feel like the most worthless pirate ever.

"You're exhausted. Let me do that," Frankie says, and gestures for me to get out of the seat. "You pull the sand away as I dig."

We switch places and continue this process until the hole is so big, we have to slide the digger down inside it and work in circles. This proves to be pretty tricky, but between us we slide it down and get it repositioned so Frankie can work it again. And we keep digging and pushing and moving and piling the sand. I've seen enough sand at this point to never go to the beach again. I don't think I can take any more.

"That's enough."

Frankie stops and looks at me. "What?"

"It's enough. I'm done." I kick the sand and it sprays everywhere. "There's nothing here!"

"Savvy, are you okay?"

I'm not okay but I don't know how to explain it to Frankie. I sink to my knees in the sand. I want to punch it. I want to punch everything. Grandpa made this too hard. Which makes me think either I misunderstood or . . . he *wasn't* right about the treasure.

"Savannah, what's going on?"

Words aren't even making sense in my mind. I shake my head. "Nothing's going on. This is all fake. Just a game. Grandpa wouldn't have set us up like this! I was wrong."

Frankie comes over and sits in the sand next to me.

"Go ahead and say it!" I yell at her. Tears run down my sandy cheeks. I try to wipe them away but they don't stop. "Go ahead and say you told me so! I'm so stupid."

Frankie leans closer to me. "You are not, Savannah Mae. You are the last person in the world I would call stupid. Why would you even think that?"

"Because I fell for it. I wanted Grandpa's map to be real. I wanted the treasure to be real. I did so much for him! I skipped school, I lied to Mom and Dad. And there's nothing here!"

I'm hot inside, like melting, burning hot. So mad at Grandpa for setting me up. So mad at him for trying to make me believe in magic. "He died and left nothing here! He's a liar."

"You know that's not true." Frankie's crying now too, but her voice is serious. "He'd never lie to us, not even for a game. I was wrong to think that."

"What are we going to do, Frankie? We have nothing to save the Queen Mary. We're going to have to move, and everything Grandpa ever found will go to Throop."

"We can stop, if you really want to, Savvy." Frankie wipes her face. "But if there's anything I know about you, it's that you never give up. And I mean never. Remember when you were seven and wanted that little wooden ship Grandpa had made?"

"The one in the glass case?" I giggle through my tears because I know the story she's going to tell.

"Yes. The glass case that you slept next to, on the floor, protesting that you'd never go to sleep until the ship was in your room."

Laughing and crying at the same time, I look up at the starless sky. I was fascinated by that model and wanted to figure it out, wanted to understand how Grandpa built it, how he carved every little intricate sail and rope and board. "And I fell asleep in Grandpa's office."

"And after three nights of that Grandpa finally said you could have it when you turned twelve."

I smile. "Yeah. I won. I forgot all about that. I'll be twelve in October. What ever happened to that ship?"

"I don't know, that's not the point. But what I do know is that you always win, Savvy. When it's important to you. I don't know if there's a treasure here; I don't know if we've got it right. But I know you can't quit until you know for sure, or until Mom and Dad drag us away, otherwise you're going to always wonder."

"Yeah." My arms and back ache so bad but Frankie is right. I'll never stop wondering if I don't keep trying. And thoughts of Dunmore Throop coming out here and finding the treasure first make me stand up and brush the sand off my legs. If there is something here, he is *not* getting it. Grandpa clearly went to great lengths to hide whatever it is from him.

"All right. Let's keep going."

"Okay." She gets up and goes back to her post. I get ready to move sand as quickly as possible, but first I look up at my big sister and she's a strong and beautiful silhouette against faraway lightning in the dark woods. Sometimes she makes me really mad, but I don't know what I'd do without her.

"Thanks, Frankie."

Frankie waves at me like I'm silly and then pulls the handles back, lifts the sand, dumps the sand. Pulls the handles back, lifts the sand, dumps the sand. Over and over and over. I use both hands to pull as much away as possible to clear the area for her to keep digging. We do this for what feels like forever without even thinking while the lightning flashes on around us. Eventually thunder follows, a slight deep rumble somewhere far away, like it might even be underground.

The digging becomes motions to do over and over and over, memorized like a dance, until suddenly . . .

Suddenly my fingers feel something other than sand.

"Wait, wait, wait! *Stop!*" I shout. "There's something here."

Frankie jumps down off the seat and joins me. My heart pounds against my ribs as I dig around the object with my fingers. I can't possibly dig fast enough. There's a fringe of fabric poking up through the ground. I tug at it, but it's held fast.

"What do you think it is?" I ask as I scratch around the edges.

"Kind of strange, but it looks like burlap, maybe?" Frankie whispers. She's very close to me, our sandy arms touching as we both pull at it. The fabric releases a tiny bit, but is still held down too deep. "I'm not sure. Let's use our hands so we don't damage anything."

Gently we scratch around the fabric to get rid of extra sand, carefully excavating the burlap until we have a huge section of it out and can see it has words printed on it. I can hardly breathe. "What is it?"

"Something Costa Rica?" Frankie guesses. "This looks like a coffee sack like Dawn's mom has at her café, those big burlap bags the beans come in."

"All we found is trash?" My voice cracks on "trash." I don't know if I can take it. "That's not old! And it's definitely not treasure! Coffee is disgusting!"

"Calm down. We still have a ways to go, this is only a small section. Keep digging until we can pull it all the way out."

My shoulders are screaming, my back feels like it's bent the wrong way, my fingernails are cracked and filled with sand and now we've spent all this time digging up someone's garbage? I want to scream at Frankie for agreeing to do this with me. I want to scream at

Grandpa for making this so complicated. Mostly I just want to scream.

But I don't. I keep digging. Just like Frankie said.

Slowly, slowly, we uncover the burlap bag, gently pulling sections of it out at a time, the sand falling away in clumps, until it's almost free from the ground. I stand up and hold it for Frankie and me to see: COSTA RICA, 1990, MAGIC BEAN COFFEE printed across the front.

Definitely not treasure.

I feel like I'm going to melt right into the ground. But Frankie's words keep me going. I tug out the last corner of the bag, which is still anchored in the sand, with my last bit of strength.

There's something small but very heavy inside.

Definitely not coffee beans.

Dead Men Tell No Tales

I turn the bag until I find an opening, and then slide the object out onto the ground. It's wrapped in more burlap.

"It's really heavy," I say as I pick it up and begin to unwrap.

"What is it?" Frankie asks. "Hurry up!" Thunder—closer, louder—seems to echo her.

"I'm trying!" I unwind and unwind until a fat skeleton key and a tiny scroll of paper fall out. "A key?" I show Frankie, confused at what we've found.

It looks like it's made out of gold. She dusts off sand to reveal red and green jewels all around the intricate handle. "It's so pretty," she says. "Do you think it's real?"

"A real key?" I ask. "Like for a real door?"

"No, real gold and whatever these gems are! It looks like it's worth a lot!"

"I'm still trying to figure out why it's a key and not a

treasure chest," I say, even though I knew a chest wasn't likely. Though the key is really cool, I feel like I've been tricked. This can't possibly be Blackbeard's treasure.

"Maybe it's a key *to* a treasure chest," Frankie whispers. "What's the little paper?"

I unravel the scroll, which reveals another code. This time there's no letters, just a ton of dots and dashes. It's Morse code.

She puts a hand to her forehead. "Grandpa, what were you thinking . . ."

"We should have known," I say.

"So Mom and Dad were right." Frankie's shoulders slump. "It is a game."

"No," I say. "I don't think so. Remember his poem said something about treasures all over town? I think he hid clues with parts of the treasure all over town so Throop wouldn't find it. This is going to lead us to something bigger. I just know it."

"And Throop's covering all the bases—following us and trying to get the house, too," Frankie says. "This is so much bigger than we thought, Sav."

"So you think this key opens a chest after all?" It would definitely be way easier if that was the case.

"Maybe, but knowing Grandpa that's too easy. I think this opens a door somewhere. Maybe for the next clue," Frankie says. "Maybe this little code will tell us where? Can you solve it, Sav?"

"Not here. But it's easy enough. I need Grandpa's Morse code book. It's still in the study at home."

Frankie claps her hands under her chin. "I bet once we figure out all the clues and find whatever's hidden at each spot, we will have to put them together to find the main treasure location."

"Why didn't he get the treasure himself, then, if he knew where it was?" I say, exasperated.

"Maybe he ran out of time? But maybe he knew we could reach it, with the right clues?"

"That sounds about right." The voice cuts through the night like a sail ripping across the sea.

Throop.

We both startle and gasp. Frankie hides the key behind her back. For a moment he's only a voice. We look around wildly to see what direction he's coming from but there's nothing but dark tree shadows.

"Where are you?" I yell. And then, like the universe is trying to help us, a flash lights up the woods and we see him. With Peter standing right next to him. "Peter Dare! Did you tattle on us? Traitor!" But he looks pale and frightened and I realize I'm wrong.

Throop must have caught Peter on the way out.

Throop talks before Peter can say anything. "It truly was genius, after all, leaving the fate of an ancient legendary treasure in the hands of two small, unsuspecting little girls, thinking his secrets would be safe with you.

Either a genius or completely insane." Throop laughs. It's a sound I'll never get out of my head as long as I live.

The laugh of a desperate man.

He smiles with thin, nearly invisible lips and digs his long fingers into Peter's shoulder. Peter winces.

"Let my cousin go!" I pick up a shovel and point it at Throop like a sword.

"Your family bonds are simply touching. No worries. I intend to do exactly that. After you hand me whatever it is you found in the bag. I couldn't quite see from this vantage point."

"The bag was empty," Frankie says. I think she sounds convincing but Dunmore Throop shrugs.

"Suit yourself." He turns with Peter still under his grip and starts to walk toward the beach rather than the road. He must have a boat anchored out there, and that's how he's been snooping around so much and so quickly. I wonder where he could possibly be going. But I don't have time to think about it because he's trying to steal our cousin!

"Wait!" Frankie says. "You can't take him. That's kidnapping!"

"I'm well aware," Throop says. I'm pretty sure he rolls his eyes. "But I'll be off this island before you even get home and who's going to believe two little treasure-hunting misfit girls like you?"

Peter sniffs.

I can't tell if Throop is serious about taking Peter or

if he's only trying to scare us, which is working. But I can tell Peter's going to start crying any second and I can't bear that. I grab the key from Frankie's hands and hold it up.

"Savannah! No!" she scolds me, but I have a plan.

"You want it?" I say to Throop. "Let him go first or I'm running this straight out to the ocean. You can't chase me and hold him at the same time."

"Now let's not be hasty," he says, a grin spreading across his face. "You can't outrun me."

"How do you know?" I have to shout over a loud rumble of thunder. The storm is getting closer and making me nervous, but not as much as Throop makes me nervous.

He fidgets a little bit, like the thunder unnerves him too. And then he makes his biggest mistake.

He lets Peter go.

I yell, "Everybody run!"

Thar She Blows!

Frankie and Peter glance at me for less than a second and run in opposite directions. They don't know my plan, but realize quickly that Throop can't catch all of us. I dash farther into the woods, leaping over branches, ducking under draped moss, with my fingers wrapped tightly around the key. Throop is loud as he crashes through the brush after me, and he doesn't know the woods like I do. He'll never catch up. I turn back and run in the direction Frankie went, listening carefully for her quieter footsteps between the thunder and *pat-pat-pat* of fat raindrops starting to hit the sand. I catch up to her quickly.

"Oh my gosh, you scared me, Savvy!"

I hold my finger to my lips and hand off the key. "Go straight home," I whisper through haggard breaths. "I'll meet you there." She tries to ask me where I'm going, but I turn back the way I came without answering.

"Savvy! There's a storm coming!"

But I keep going.

Straight to the beach, because I know that's where Throop will go.

The storm is over us, but still hasn't let loose its full power. The ghost crabs scuttle out of my way and into their little holes in the sand to escape the rain as I break through the underbrush and stumble out onto the beach. I trip and my knees hit the sand. Catching my breath, I listen carefully for Throop, but only hear the now-violent crashing of the bay waters upon the beach between bursts of thunder. Way up on my right, there's a small motorboat pulled up onto the sand.

I knew it. He'd been sneaking around the island by boat, probably watching us to see where we were going. There are many points along the island where you can see the village from the water. People are always waving to us from the bay when we're walking around certain parts of town. I inspect Throop's boat for any clues or personal belongings of his, something to prove my point that he's up to no good, but it's completely empty. Throop's not that easy to fool. But neither am I. I'll find a way to prove to my parents that he's up to something bad.

This is the worst place I could be in a thunderstorm, and I've got to get home. But there's a scuffling sound behind me, feet in sand. I spin to see Throop trying to sneak down the beach toward me. Just then the clouds open up and the fat drops turn to sharp needles. We're both soaked in seconds.

"I see you!" I yell through the noise and keep my hands behind my back, pretending I'm still hiding the key.

"You stay right there, young lady," Throop says, holding a finger up and squinting like he might lose sight of me in the rain.

Cold settles in my bones, the rain stabs at my skin. It's miserable. I raise my hand up in the air, as if I'm going to throw something into the water. "Don't come any closer."

"Throw it if you like, little miss," Throop says. "You've already done the hard work of unraveling the old man's clues. I should have known his sentimentality would make him tie this all to you girls. I can surely find a key in a shallow bay." But he stops walking anyway. Crosses his arms across his chest. I do the same. Two pirates in a duel. The rain feels like needles on my face.

"You said you didn't know what was in the bag."

"I lied."

"It doesn't belong to you," I shout over the thunder.

"Yes, actually, it does."

"How?"

Throop laughs and looks around at the whipping branches and sheets of rain. "Hardly the time to explain it to a child!"

"I'm not afraid of a little rain. Besides, you're taller than me. The lightning will go for you first!" I shout. "So explain!"

"Look. I don't want to hurt you or your sisters or your family, but Cornelius should have known I'd come back for what I rightfully gained. He had no right leaving this to children."

I keep my feet planted in the sand, which keeps shifting with the soaking rain, but my knees are bent, ready to run at a moment's notice. "I'm not giving you anything without an explanation," I say.

Throop takes his hat off and pushes his sopping hair out of his face before he puts his hat back on. "Years ago, Cornelius and I were looking for the *Queen Anne's Revenge* together. Do you know what that is?"

"Of course I know what that is! It's one of Blackbeard's boats!" I yell. Any member of the Dare family would know this. "He ran it aground to escape capture and it's never been found," I say as the rain pelts my face. But it doesn't sting as much as the realization just that moment that *that's* what "QAR" stands for. The ship! And the clue was on the walking stick all this time.

"You're the smart one," Throop says. "Cornelius told me. I forgot." He looks out at the horizon in the direction the storm is quickly moving toward. I nearly jump out of my spot to run away, but I have to know more, so I force my feet to stay still, reminding myself the key is safe with Frankie. Even though I'm not.

"Anyway?" I yell impatiently. "You haven't convinced me anything belongs to you."

"We were a team for several years. We found many artifacts including that key, which your grand-father believed went to something on the *Queen Anne's Revenge*. A locked box, maybe a little cupboard, that one of Blackbeard's crew stole and carried off the ship before it sank. I didn't agree about the treasure but wanted to help the old man find the shipwreck. Because that would be joint investment, joint profit. See what I'm saying?"

"Yes." I no longer need to shout as the rain is dying down, and the thunder and lightning follow the clouds across the bay.

"Somewhere along the line, your grandfather didn't think my motives were 'pure,'" Throop says, making air quotes on "pure." "He foolishly believed everything we found belonged in a museum. But treasure hunters don't hunt treasure to lock it up behind a glass case simply for people to drag their sniveling children by it."

"You wanted to sell everything and be rich and famous. And he didn't," I say. I can understand both Grandpa's point *and* Throop's, which kind of scares me. Why shouldn't a treasure hunter get something out of all their hard work?

"I wanted to sell that key and use the money to keep looking for the ship. But your grandfather insisted it was part of a greater treasure. He put an end to the hunt for the *Queen Anne's Revenge* and kept all the research we'd done for himself."

Throop might be telling the truth, I think. He's very convincing and obviously Grandpa did have at least one of Throop's books. If Grandpa was right, the ship and the bigger treasure are still out there. But if Throop is right, and the key is all there is, and it's worth a lot by itself, I want to sell it to save our house. We could give Throop and Uncle Randy the money and keep our home.

Grandpa, I'm so sorry.

Throop takes a few steps closer. He looks like a drowned giraffe.

"So you see, lass, we can work together."

"How do I know I can trust you?"

"Give me the key and I'll leave your house alone. I promise."

I shake my head. Little does he know I don't even have the key. But something still doesn't make sense— the conversation Peter heard about Throop wanting something inside our house. "No, I'm taking it home. My parents will know what to do with it."

Throop lunges toward me, and I run faster than I ever knew I could run, back into the woods, dripping with the quick end-of-summer storm, toward the slight orange hint of the sunrise. Although a couple of times I find myself doubling back on my own footprints, eventually I break through the woods into the road by the clumps of grasses and post and rail fence that line the park.

I lean on my thighs and catch my breath, looking up and down the street, but I don't see Frankie or Peter. I have no idea if either of them has made it out of the woods and gone home or what.

"What am I supposed to do now?" I ask the empty street. Frankie could be home cozy in our attic right now waiting for me or she could still be zigzagging through the trails. My plan seemed like a good idea in the moment, but I didn't think it through to the end. I can't leave her or Peter here if they're still in the park somewhere. But I don't have a second to decide, because all of a sudden there are strong arms wrapped around my middle and I'm lifted off my feet.

"Where do you think you're going?" Throop asks, sounding amused and as if he's better than me, better than all of us.

"Nowhere with you, you scurvy dog!" I shout and squirm and kick, but I can't get free from him. He laughs that cold, desperate laugh at me.

"It's not really you kids I want anyway, lass. I told you. Just the key."

"I don't have it!"

Throop puts me down and finally sees my empty hands. His eyes narrow into slits that match his non-existent lips. And that's when I fear for my life.

"Where is it?" he roars.

"It's already safe at home and you can't touch it!" I scream at him. Then I almost run off down the street, but suddenly Frankie bursts through the bushes, also soaking wet, gasping and stumbling into the street.

And the key is gripped tightly in her hand.

Blow the Man Down!

"Get away from my sister," Frankie says.

"Don't give him the key!" I shout. Throop grabs my arm. "Run home, Frankie!"

"The two of you are something else," Throop says, still sounding like he thinks this is all a fun game that he's going to win. And then Peter comes bounding out of the woods, and we are right back where we started. I wonder if Throop is right. Only instead of sticking around and helping us, Peter takes one look and runs faster than I've ever seen him move in his life.

"So much for defending your honor," Throop says. "Now listen, girls, I have a better trade. Let me have the key and I'll make sure your house is untouchable. I'll make sure your parents don't ever have to sell it."

My heart beats a little faster. But I don't believe he's telling us the truth.

"You're just telling us what we want to hear," Frankie says. "We'll keep the key and then we won't have to sell the house anyway."

"I can buy your home and ensure you never have to leave regardless of treasure, no treasure, key or no key."

"Don't believe him, Frankie." I try to pull my arm out of his tight grasp but I can't. "He's lying!"

"Be still," he says, tightening his hand even more.

Footsteps and voices reach us before I can see who it is, and all of a sudden Throop's hand leaves my arm.

And then I see what he's looking at. A group of people rush toward us, with the cresting sun behind them; only their dark silhouettes give them away. As they get closer, I realize it's my parents, Peter and his parents, and Jolene.

"Oh, you're done for now, Throop!" I say, backing away from him as quickly as I can.

Jolene rushes up to Frankie and me, and hugs us quickly before she turns on Throop. "You stay away from my sisters, you scallywag!" She lunges at the confused man. I have to say, with that eye patch Jolene does look pretty fierce. Even in her footie pajamas.

"What's going on here?" My dad grabs ahold of Jolene before she can bite Throop. Throop's expression has changed completely. I don't know how he does it! Instead of looking like a squinty-eyed madman, he looks like our friendly mailman.

"I was only helping the girls find their way out of the woods, Jack," Throop lies, his voice now quieter, but still like he thinks he's better than everyone else.

"It's not true, Dad," I yell. "Don't believe him."

Before my dad or anyone can react, Throop tips his green hat. "I'll be on my way now that everyone is safe and sound."

"Wait a second there, bud," Uncle Randy says. "You're in the woods in the middle of the night with my son and my nieces and you think you're going to walk away with no questions asked?" He grabs on to Throop's arm like Throop did to me. "We've already called the sheriff. You're waiting right here."

Throop rips his arm out of Uncle Randy's grasp. But he keeps his voice calm. He hands Uncle Randy one of his cards. "Call me tomorrow and we will straighten everything out. Everyone's safe and sound and that's all that matters." He walks briskly down the street opposite the sunrise, into the darkness.

"What a weirdo," Peter says, his clothes dripping on the street.

My dad looks at us. "You're all okay? Right, girls? He didn't hurt you, did he?" He turns our faces to see if there are any scratches or anything. We shake our heads and before I can tell them all the stuff Throop said, Officer Howard shows up and asks us all a bunch of questions about Throop, like what he was wearing and what he wanted, which we have to pretend we don't know.

"What were y'all doing out here so late anyway?" he asks when he's done.

"Playing manhunt," Peter lies. For the first time ever.

The grown-ups tell Officer Howard which way Throop went and he tells us to head home. He'll call us in the morning with any news.

"We had this guy all wrong," Uncle Randy says as we walk back. "We owe you all an apology." He puts his hand on Dad's shoulder.

"It's okay," Dad says. "I know you were trying to help."

"Good news is I don't think he'll be back," Uncle Randy says.

"What makes you say that?" Mom asks.

"He's way outnumbered, first of all. And he just got run out of town by a band of local pirates." Uncle Randy grins at us.

"Don't encourage them, Randy," Aunt Della says.

Frankie and I look at each other. There really are no words. Except to thank our cousin.

"Thank you, Peter," Frankie says.

"Yeah, you saved our butts," I say. "Thank you so much!"

"It's fine," he says. "We're family. That's what we do for each other."

Before I can say anything more about the key or the conversation on the beach, Mom launches into frantic full-question mode.

"What in the world were you three doing out here anyway? You weren't actually playing manhunt this late at night, were you?" she asks. "Jolene woke us up, said Peter was soaking wet and knocking on the door and told her there was trouble in the park. I thought someone had drowned. What were you all thinking? Were you out here all night long?"

Frankie gets right to the point. She holds up the key. "Grandpa's treasure is real."

The adults get into all-out question mode after that. And we tell them everything we know. So far. No more secrets.

We walk home while they pass the key between them and talk like excited kids.

"There's something familiar about this," Dad says, and they all examine and discuss and argue about the key. Something about Spanish gold in the 1700s and where the emeralds and rubies might be from, why Grandpa would bury something so valuable in the park, and how Throop knew about it. I know the answer, but none of us can get a word in while the grown-ups talk.

They'll figure it out.

Frankie, Jolene, Peter, and I trail behind. Jolene asks us a million questions about how we finally found it. She's wide-awake because she's been sleeping for the last however many hours we've been working our butts off. But I'm so tired I can't think straight anymore. Too many questions and too much sand. My clothes stick to my skin and it's itchy and cold.

I try to answer some of Jolene's questions but my words come out in mixed-up sounds, like I can't remember what order they're supposed to be in.

"Savvy, are you okay?" Frankie asks.

I feel like I'm sinking underwater. She holds me up.

Before we even get back to the house, I hear Frankie say, "Um, Dad?"

She sounds very far away.

And then I somehow end up in my dad's arms and the last thing I remember is him tucking me into bed.

26

The Family That Pirates Together

When I wake up, I feel like I've eaten all the sand from the beach. My mouth is swollen and stuck together and my skin is dry like the paper in Grandpa's old books. Even my eyeballs feel dried out. Sand falls out onto my pillow when I scratch my head. Gross.

Next to my bed is a little pitcher of water and a glass my mom must have left for me. I pour myself a drink and then another and then pull my heavy arms and legs out of bed to take a shower. The hot water feels so good washing away the salt and dirt down the drain. When I get back to my room, my mom has stripped my bed and laid out clean clothes for me. Normally I'd roll my eyes at that. I'm not a baby. But today I'm thankful for one less thing to think about.

Downstairs, Mom and Dad are reading through one

of Grandpa's journals that I kept. When they see me, they toss the book on the table and smile.

"Good to see you up, Savvy," Dad says, extending an arm out for me to sit next to them on the couch. I lean into his warm side.

"What time is it? Where's Frankie and Jolene?"

"It's around two," Mom says, looking at her watch. "And your sisters are out walking Py. They should be back soon."

"Two?" I ask. "Two in the afternoon? I missed breakfast *and* lunch?"

Mom laughs. "Yes, but I can make you a sandwich if you're hungry?"

"I don't even know yet."

"Well, you're very dehydrated, so I'm going to at least get you more water."

I nod and Dad gives me a squeeze. Everything from last night starts popping into my head, like I'd forgotten it for a bit, and now it's like little light bulbs brightening the room one at a time. Digging, Throop, running all over the woods, a gold key, a thunderstorm, passing out in Frankie's arms.

"The key?"

"Right now, the key is safe and sound," Dad says, gently pinching my nose.

"What are you going to do with it?" I ask.

"Well, we want to find the right expert to evaluate it.

Although your mom and I do believe it's from the 1700s, our knowledge is limited. We'd need to comb through all of Grandpa's records to see if he has anything about its origin. It's going to take time. And there's the little issue of the government."

"What do you mean?"

"It's tricky," Dad says, "because you and your sisters were digging on state land, so therefore it technically belongs to the state."

"But it already belonged to Grandpa. He put it there for us to find," I say. To unlock an even bigger treasure, I think, but don't say out loud to my dad.

"Can't prove to anyone that it belonged to him, Savvy. It would be different if you found it in our yard, or if you had a permit to treasure hunt like your grandpa used to have. And no matter what, the state can claim a certain amount of any artifacts found by a private treasure hunter—that's something your grandfather always had to work with, too.

"So, for right now, we're going to keep it safe and try to find out as much as we can," he says. "And then we can make a better decision on what to do with it."

Mom comes back with a glass of water and some cinnamon toast for me. She kisses the top of my head. "What are you grinning at?" she asks.

"I never knew my parents were such good pirates."

"Let's not go too far," Mom says, smiling.

"But you believe us now, that Blackbeard's treasure is out there?" I ask them.

"That's still up for debate," Dad says. "Hear me out, before you argue."

"Okay."

"I believe that Grandpa believed it was out there. I believe he set up this wonderful hunt for you girls before he died because he loved stuff like this, and knew you would, too. But he wasn't thinking clearly the last several years, Savvy. If he had been, he'd never have risked you digging on state land like this. Do you understand what I'm saying?"

"I think so," I say. "Grandpa wouldn't want us doing anything dangerous. Or illegal."

Dad rubs my back. "Exactly."

"Are you going to make us stop?"

Dad takes a long, deep breath. "I'm not. Because the other part of this is the fact that this key is not a toy. It's the real deal and I can't believe my father's judgment was so bad he'd bury something like this in the park." He shuts his eyes and rubs his temples. "Anyway, I want you to let Mom and I know where you are at all times. If you think you have an idea where something else might be, you let us know. And especially if Dunmore Throop shows up again." Dad grits his teeth at Throop's name.

"Okay." I can deal with that. Even pirates had a code, like Frankie said.

My sisters come in the front door and Py breaks free from Jolene's hand, runs up to me, and jumps up on my knees. I give her a good scratch. Jolene comes over and hugs me. "I thought you might never wake up," she says. I hug her.

"We stopped by Peter's house," Frankie says. "He and Uncle Randy went to the park to get Will's backhoe and fill the hole in so no one gets hurt."

"Oh, good," Mom says. "Della told me they were going to do that. Glad they took care of it."

Now there was no trace of what we'd done.

I guess Uncle Randy and Peter might make good pirates too. The vote's still out on that.

"All right, Savannah, your orders are to rest for the next couple of days," Mom says. "You're lucky you're not grounded for a month for skipping school."

"Frankie told you."

"Sorry, Sav," Frankie says. "Mom made me walk the plank."

"Yes, Frankie told me. She had little choice when you passed out. You scared us. But she told me what all was going on this week and it was obvious that you needed a lot of rest and water. So that's what you're getting."

"Okay."

"And your first order of business is this." She hands me a stack of Grandpa's books.

"You want me to see what I can find out about the key?"

She pinches my nose just like Dad. "Smart as a whip."

What could be better? This is like the opposite of getting grounded. I get to lie on the couch and go through Grandpa's things to try to figure out where the key fits and where it came from!

"Don't get too cozy," she says. "You're going back on Monday."

Surprisingly, I'm not actually sad about it. Mom and Dad both agree that we're not sending all of Grandpa's things away after all, because we have to find out what else Grandpa hid in town and we need his research. So the key is safe and sound. Things are mostly good.

Except that we still haven't figured out how to save the Queen Mary.

For She's a Jolly Good Fellow

We roll through leaves on the way to school on Monday, and when we get there, kids surround our skateboards. Everyone has heard something different about what happened that night with Throop.

"My dad says you took down a bank robber at the beach," one boy says.

"I heard someone was trying to break into the lighthouse," another kid says.

"That's not it at all," says a girl from Frankie's class. "My mom said someone had been snooping around all week at the museum and Sheriff Howard caught him while they were playing manhunt in the park."

Frankie, Jolene, and I look at each other. "Yeah," Frankie says. "That's close enough."

But all day the questions continue. I stick to the

manhunt story. At lunch a lot of kids ask to eat with me, but there's someone I have to find.

When I see Kate, I ask if I can sit with her and LouAnn.

"Sure," she says. "If you really want to."

"I do."

They both watch me sit and unpack my lunch. Neither asks me anything about the night at the park or why I'm suddenly talking to them. We eat in silence for a minute until Grandpa's words force me to talk.

"Kate?"

"Yeah?"

"Let's call a parley."

"A what?"

"A truce," I explain. "I'm really sorry I pushed you last year."

"Oh, it's okay!" She grins and sets down her turkey sandwich. "I know you were just angry. I shouldn't have called you weird."

"With chicken legs," LouAnn adds.

"Right." Kate stops chewing and looks at the table. "I don't know why I said that. I'm really sorry too. Let's not fight again."

"Okay."

I don't tell them about moving and they don't ask me any questions about what happened with Throop. We talk about school and friends and we trade desserts.

It's like nothing bad ever happened between us. I guess Grandpa was right, everyone needed to grow up a little bit. Saying sorry wasn't really that hard and now everything feels back to normal.

Every day after school I continue to read through Grandpa's journals, but don't find anything about the key. And then one day we come home to a FOR SALE sign in our front yard.

At dinner that night Mom says that the real estate agent wants us to clear out the house and put everything in storage before she starts showing it to potential buyers. "She says too much clutter will discourage them."

"No way," Dad says. "People are going to have to use their imaginations. The only place all of these treasures are going is a museum, and only when we are ready."

I think it's the first time Dad has called Grandpa's things "treasures."

"The Grandpa Museum," Jolene says, pushing little halves of cherry tomatoes around on her plate.

"The what?" Dad asks, chuckling over his glass of water.

"We think Grandpa should have his own museum. With his name on a banner and everything," I say. "He deserves it."

Dad's eyes get all watery. I look down at my plate.

He squeezes my hand. "That's a lovely idea, Savvy. You girls always believed in him way more than I ever did."

He gets up and leaves the table.

I look over at Mom. "It's okay, sweetheart," she says.

"You didn't do anything wrong." Then she gets up and follows Dad.

Jolene pushes her eye patch up onto her head and taps her fork on her plate. Py walks around under the table waiting for us to drop something. She curls up at my feet when she comes up empty.

"I guess we should be happy," Frankie says, her chin scrunched in her hand. "Even though it's not going to save the house, we proved Grandpa was right."

"Yeah, but we can't even tell anybody," Jolene says.

"I know. But we know. We proved it to ourselves." Frankie gathers our plates, scrapes all the food onto one, and piles them up. It's obvious we're all done eating even though we never started. I grab a small piece of chicken and hand it to Py under the table.

"But the thing is, there's still more to find," I say. "And now we have to leave."

"Maybe every time someone comes to look at the house, we can say that it's haunted and how horrible it is to live here," Jolene suggests. It's not a bad idea.

"Maybe we'll just get lucky and no one will even want it right away," Frankie says. "It could buy Mom and Dad enough time to figure out the key." But it doesn't make me feel any better.

I rest my head on the table. We solved a huge piece of Grandpa's puzzle, but we might not have enough time to solve the whole thing. And what if Dunmore Throop comes back in the meantime? No one has heard anything from him. The police said they'd keep a lookout and would bring him in for questioning if he ever comes back but they never found him that night. Mom wanted to know why they couldn't do more.

"Unless there's actually a crime, they can't charge him for yelling at kids," Dad had told her.

I reach down and give the dog a scratch. She has such an easy life. All she ever has to think about is food and scratches.

Then the doorbell rings.

Jolene runs to it and peeks out the window. "It's Mrs. Taylor. Can I open it?"

"Of course," Frankie says, and we join Jolene at the door. Mrs. Taylor looks like she got caught in a wind tunnel.

"Girls!" she says, breathless. "I have a plan!"

"A plan for what, ma'am?" Frankie asks, and plucks a leaf out of Mrs. Taylor's hair.

"Your home! I did a little research. The Queen Mary qualifies for registration on the historical database. I'm sure you'd be approved to stay as caretakers. The council agreed they didn't want just anyone to own such an important part of Ocracoke's history, for fear they might tear it down and build something atrocious. So now all your parents have to do is take it from here!"

She holds up a paper for us to see. It looks very formal and all, but I'm not sure if it matters anymore. "Mrs. Taylor, they already put our house up for sale."

She turns and looks at the sign out front. "Well, you won't be needing that anymore!" And then Mrs. Taylor does something very unexpected.

She rushes over to the sign and kicks it over.

Jolene gasps. "Shiver me timbers!"

"Mom! Dad!" Jolene yells up the stairs so loud the dog runs under the dining room table. "Mrs. Taylor says we can be carebakers and won't have to move!"

"Caretakers," Frankie corrects her.

"That's what I said," Jolene says.

"Don't be too hasty. You at least don't have to sell *yet*," Mrs. Taylor says. "I'll explain when your parents get down here."

When our parents don't reappear immediately, Jolene yells, "Jack and Anne Dare, your presence is requested in the captain's quarters!"

"Jolene, what is all the commotion?" Mom says, appearing at the top of the landing. "Oh, Mrs. Taylor, hello. Is everything all right?"

"Anne, everything is far better than all right."

We all sit down with Mrs. Taylor in the dining room and she explains that when a house is accepted into the registry, it puts all kinds of rules in place, but the best thing about it is that the owners can ask the town council to protect their home.

"If the council votes to protect the building, it can't be torn down and you can apply for money to help keep it yourselves," she says.

"That's wonderful," Mom says. "But do we even have time to ask the council?"

"I already did. Informally." Mrs. Taylor clasps her hands and smiles. "When Savannah told me about what was happening, I decided to look into the possibility. I knew you all had a lot on your plate so I did some digging for you. Everyone is ready to vote YES! You just have to say the word and get the paperwork rolling."

Mom and Dad look at each other. Dad says, "You're going to help us keep our home?"

"I'm certainly going to try!" Mrs. Taylor nods so hard it looks like she might knock the bun off the top of her head. She rubs her hands together. "*And*, we've decided to cover your bills for two months. This will give you time to finalize the registration and apply for a grant from the government to be stewards of the property yourselves." She passes the papers to our parents and smiles at my sisters and me. "Meaning, you will be the right and true guardians of a very important historical property."

Frankie and Jolene look at me. "What did you say, Mrs. Taylor?" I ask.

"You are 'the right and true guardians'?" she repeats.

I don't know how she knows, but my sisters and I look at each other and I know they're thinking what I'm thinking.

When in doubt, please remember:
I'm with you always and forever.

196

It's like Grandpa had his hands in this all along.

"What do you think, Jack?" Mom says, after they read over the paperwork.

"I think we'll have to pinch and cut back on some things, but I know we can make it work," my dad says. "It's definitely worth a shot."

"Evelyn, thank you so much. It's exactly what we needed. A little more time." Mom sits back and sighs, and shakes her head at me.

"What?"

When she gives me that look, I always feel like I'm getting into trouble. But this time there's no eyebrow talking.

"I'm amazed at what you and your sisters have accomplished," she says. "You all believed when the rest of us couldn't do it anymore. You took on Grandpa's challenge and proved him right. And Savannah, you've saved our home simply by being you and speaking up to Mrs. Taylor at the right time. I'm amazed. And grateful."

Simply by being me, which Frankie said is just like Grandpa.

I look around the table at my family, Mrs. Taylor, and even Py, who's staring up at me with her head cocked like she's wondering what the wet stuff on my cheeks is.

"Are you *crying*?" Frankie asks, and leans toward me.

I wipe off my face as fast as I can. Pirates don't cry. Pirates fight.

My sisters gather around me and squeeze me tight.

But for today, I suppose the fight is over.

The right and true guardians have won.

On the wall across the dining room, I'm sure the portrait of Grandpa just gave me a wink.

Epilogue
One More Sign

October 1996

Frankie lights one last candle as we sit down around the Star Board. I have the Morse code message Grandpa left us with the key. It was really easy to solve once I found his book, and although I promised Dad I'd keep him posted on our explorations, I haven't said anything to him about this clue. What could it hurt to keep one little secret?

.-- .... .- - / .- -. -.-. .. . -. - / .. -. ...- . -. - .. --- -. / .- .-.. .-..
--- .-- . -.. / .--. . --- .--. .-. . / - --- / ... . . / - .... .-. --- .. --. ....
/ .-- .- .-.. .-.. ... ..-..

What ancient invention allowed people to see through walls?

"A window," Frankie answers. "That makes less sense than 'elbow.'" Her face is shadowy and serious as she sits down next to Jolene and me. We're all dressed in our favorite pirate clothes and of course, Jolene has on her eye patch. Mom made her take it off so she could wash it last week, but other than that it's hardly left her face, except for when we're at school because her teacher said she's going to ruin her eyes.

"Deadlights," I say.

"What?"

"Just made me think of deadlights. They are the windows on a pirate ship. And sometimes that's what pirates called eyes—the window to the soul."

"Creepy," Jolene says.

"What do you think it means?" Frankie asks.

"No idea."

"Maybe Blackbeard can help us with this one," Jolene says. She's starting to come round to the Star Board and sits cross-legged with her back straight and her hands ready to go. She's even started memorizing some of the constellations on the chart.

"I think you're right, but you know what we need before we go any further with this treasure hunt?" I say. "Pirate names."

"Yes!" Frankie says. "I love that idea. What should we use?"

"Well, Edward Teach went by Blackbeard because he had a huge black beard, so I guess we should use things that describe us," I say.

Jolene sits up even straighter. "Then I'm One-Eyed Wonder, like Peter said."

"I like it," I say. "Frankie?"

She thinks for a moment. "From now on you can call me Frankie 'Sycamore' Dare."

We all laugh at that one. That lady with the funny accent from New Jersey had it right. Frankie *is* tall.

"What about you?" Jolene asks me. "What do you want to be called?"

"Savvy," I say.

"But that's already your name," says Jolene.

"Exactly. 'Cause I've been a pirate all along." Only Grandpa knew it.

"Perfect," Frankie says. "Savvy Savannah is perfect."

"No one can mess with Frankie Sycamore Dare, Savvy Savannah Mae, and the One-Eyed Wonder." Jolene jumps on the couch, crouching with a wooden sword like she's ready for an attack. I wish Grandpa could see his pirate princess now. Then again, maybe he can.

This time, as we settle in to talk to Blackbeard, there're no questions from Frankie, and no giggling from Jolene. The crow's nest is dark but cozy, and hopefully especially welcoming to our ghostly guide. Without his help, we might not have escaped Dunmore Throop. And now we need help again.

"Edward Teach, it's us again. The right and true guardians, the Dare sisters: Frankie Sycamore Dare,

Savvy Savannah, and Jolene the One-Eyed Wonder." Jolene giggles after that, but I keep going.

"Please give us a sign that you're here, Edward," I say. Even I'm trembling a little bit, but I think it's because I'm more excited about what he might tell us, and if he knows anything else about Grandpa's remaining clues that will lead us to the final X marks the spot.

Everything stays very quiet this time, except for some creaking in the rafters. Jolene looks up, all over the ceiling, then closes her eyes—eye—and stays calm. If Blackbeard is swinging from the rafters, this time she doesn't seem to mind.

"Tell him about the key," Jolene whispers. "Tell him how you barely escaped Throop's clutches!"

"Tell him we know he's on our side now," Frankie says.

"Shhh! Only one person at a time can talk or he'll get confused!" I say. Frankie makes a face at me. "Edward, we know you're on our side now," I say. I tell Blackbeard everything that happened at Springer's Point, and how we have a key that we think belonged to him, hidden by our grandfather.

"Our grandfather wanted nothing more than to have your treasure in a museum. Now that our home is safe, we want to make that happen. We promise." My sisters nod their heads.

"May you please help us, Mr. Blackbeard?" Jolene

asks. We squeeze in closer together, our knees all touching. The paddle begins to move.

Lynx.
Eridanus.
Sagittarius.
Y
E
S

"He said 'yes'!" Jolene shouts. "He said 'yes,' he'll still help us!"

"Shhh!" I put my hand over her mouth. "Don't scare him away." I take my hand away. "But good job."

Jolene smiles and sits up straighter. "I intrepid it all by myself."

Frankie rolls her eyes. "I think you mean 'interpreted.'"

"That's what I said."

I love my pirate sisters.

Savvy and her sisters love talking like pirates.
Here are some of their favorite terms for you to practice
for National Talk Like a Pirate Day (September 19)!

The Pirate Glossary

Ahoy! .... to acknowledge another ship or person

all hands on deck .... everyone has to help

blow the man down .... to kill someone

carouser .... partygoer

crow's nest .... lookout on a ship

dead men tell no tales .... leave no witnesses

landlubber .... someone who doesn't know the sea and doesn't sail

May day! .... a call of distress from a boat

me hearties .... friends

scallywag/scalawag .... villain or mischievous person

Shiver me timbers! .... an exclamation of surprise

to go on account .... to become a pirate

X marks the spot .... place where treasure is hidden. Sometimes.

Author's Note

Ocracoke Island, along with the town of Avon up the beach a bit, harbored in my heart when I was fourteen. North Carolina's Outer Banks—their natural beauty, quiet beaches, and the unique lifestyle of their communities—became a place I knew I'd return to. I also knew I'd someday write a story set on Ocracoke, but it wasn't until I saw three sisters skateboarding in Key Largo that I had my characters. The Dare sisters have elements of all of the best women in my life, living in my favorite place, wrapped up in a story that embraces family, the close-knit community of a small town (with which I'm very familiar), pirate treasure, and a few friendly ghosts. I only hope the true residents of the village will forgive me for the many liberties I've taken with their home and my obvious disadvantage of never having lived in this special place.

Since the writing of this book, Ocracoke suffered great devastation when Hurricane Dorian hit in August 2019. Hurricanes are indeed a part of life on all barrier islands, but this storm caused more damage and flooding than any in all of Ocracoke's recent history. The Ocracoke Community Foundation has been set up for donations if you're moved to lend a hand. www.obcf.org

Acknowledgments

Cheers!

To Linda Epstein—my agent and friend. I have not had many true advocates in my life. Thank you for lighting the way.

To the editing, design, and marketing teams at Imprint, for all your hard work and belief in this book. Especially Nicole Otto—your enthusiasm for my story and love of Grandpa Cornelius will stay with me forever. And Captain John Morgan, you took over this mission with more charm and insight than I ever expected. I am so happy to continue charting this course with you.

To the academic and artistic communities that have given me confidence, skills, and support to create the life and career I dreamed about: The Allies in Wonderland, Vermont College of Fine Arts, Sierra Nevada College, the inimitable Highlights Foundation, Weymouth Center of Arts and Humanities, Bloomsburg University, and, finally, Warren County Community College—especially professors BJ Ward and Brian Bradford—where I first dipped my toes in this new, second life and immediately knew I was finally in the right ocean.

To several teachers in my high school days who saw something in me that I couldn't see, especially Louise

Edgcomb who remains a friend to this day.

To all me hearties who have read my stories or mentored my craft or simply been sailing along with me: Donna Galanti; Erica George; Kathryn Craft; Josh Horowitz; Marie and Baldev Lamba; Shane, Logan, and Sawyer McGee; Heather Pasqualino; Diana Thorn; Terry Wilson; Caroline Scutt and Jeff Trimmer; Natasha Sinel; Nicole Valentine; Nelson Giboyeaux Centeno—each one of you, a sail on this ship.

To Kim Bakke and Pablo Cartaya—two of the best first mates I have ever had in my life. I'll just leave it at that, otherwise we'll all be crying.

To the women in my family: Becca, Mom, Mema, Charlene, and Sharon—for showing me how strong women (sisters/mothers/daughters) can build each other up, rather than tear each other down, each one of you pirate queens.

To my kiddos—I know you don't totally understand why I do what I do and why I've made the choices I've made, but you three have inspired me for over two decades now (!) and in all kinds of ways you end up in my stories. Always remember the Cord of Three.

To my sweetheart Joe—you never let me forget the magic and wonder of this life for which I am eternally grateful. There is no one else with whom I want to sail this ship.

To Edward Teach, whose story (one with many liberties in itself) lives on over three hundred years after your death, a feat many writers aspire to. I like to think rather than the dramatic and violent reputation you built, it's the adventure and mystery that keeps us looking for treasure, the untold story we cling to in order to keep believing.

And finally to my Poppy, who I never got to know very well, but who believed in me unfailingly, and who I imagine would have gotten along very well with Cornelius Franklin Dare. In some strange and magical way, I picture you together smoking pipes and poring over maps. Yo-ho, a pirate's life!

About the Author

Jess Rinker always wanted to find treasure as a child. In the woods or on the beach, she was always hunting for something, and when she first visited the Outer Banks of North Carolina at fourteen she discovered the incredible history there was a treasure in itself. She could never be a pirate because she gets seasick, but writing about pirates has been quite fun. She's now a children's author and writing teacher, and she still searches for treasures. *The Dare Sisters* is her first middle grade novel.

jessrinker.com